SHERWOOD'S END

DIANE J. REED

Bandits Ranch Books

Cover design by Najla Qamber at Najla Qamber Designs, www.najlaqamberdesigns.com

This novel is dedicated to all the young lovers who never give up, and to the little old ladies in black dresses who secretly run the world…and who know what true love really means.

A candle flickers in the breeze that sneaks through the window like a thief. It swirls into the room, silent as a cat burglar, before it seeks out Skyler Worth's bare shoulders and settles on her skin. Goose bumps prickle her spray-tanned collar bones and breasts, making her shiver. The air seems a bit cold for May, with an unusual bite. Nevertheless, Skyler continues to slip off her designer underwear to prepare for bed, tossing her pink lace bra in a corner where her school uniform lays in a heap. The maids for the prestigious Pinnacle Boarding School for Girls will pick up her clothes by five the next morning and have them laundered, pressed and returned to her no later than seven. Skyler loves nothing more than watching the "help" at her high school or her parents' home in Indian Hill, Cincinnati do their jobs with a precision that rivals Victorian manor servants. Rich is as rich *does*, her mother always drilled into her—and that means taking the lead and behaving in a way that constantly reminds others of your class.

Skyler turns to her dresser to unwrap the tissue over the silk nightgown that her mother purchased for her in Paris during her annual spring shopping spree, when she feels another caress from the breeze upon her skin, only stronger this time. It lifts the strands of her long, blonde hair and tickles at her neck.

No—

More like *breathes* on it…

"Don't turn around," a low voice urges.

Skyler's breath hitches.

She hadn't heard him come in.

Her lips rise in a smile as she watches the flame dance on her lavender candle, spreading its sharp scent.

Sex night.

Skyler was hoping he'd make it. But damned if she'd let on her anticipation—

Every Wednesday, when her roommate goes to theater recital until lights out at 10 PM, and his roommate is busy tutoring the slugs in the computer lab till closing, Parker Ash, the best LaCrosse player ever to attend the neighboring Breton School for Boys, scales up the gothic wall of Skyler's wing at Pinnacle, latching his iron grip onto the chiseled marble ledges and sculpted gargoyles. Though as renowned for his brutal temper as his good looks, Parker's scholarship to Yale is assured, and so is his place as the next CEO of his father's multinational chemical manufacturing firm.

But more importantly to Skyler, Parker is a fucking god in bed.

"Close your eyes," the voice insists.

Skyler does so, loving the way he barely touches her at first. Just makes her wait, makes her yearn for him until the adrenaline snaps like electricity through her, messing with every inch of her body and brain. She feels his fingers lightly graze her skin, then trail along her shoulders and down to her slim waist, before reaching for more.

She stiffens.

"No," Skyler says, her very favorite word in the English language.

Elegance is refusal—never be too easy, her mother always warned her, even though at this moment Skyler can feel her pulse throb and moisture seep into the folds of her sex, already on fire and aching for Parker. Make sure you always get more than you ever give up, her mother insisted—that's how you rule and remain on top. These are hard-core Pinnacle values, the same Alma Mater her mother went to, and the most effective finishing school on the planet for molding high society women to dominate nearly everyone in sight.

Skyler's back straightens.

"Did you take *care* of that little business I asked you about?" she says with shards of accusation in her voice.

Though Skyler's completely naked, she knows her acid demands make her even hotter to Parker. Guys like him love a true bitch, as long as she's equally ferocious in bed—and pleasing her on all fronts can be the supreme test of his conquest. Luckily, Skyler is all of the above, and more.

Only this time, she'd really upped the ante.

Bree Mortimer is the troublesome new element who'd entered the picture—both drop-dead gorgeous and as dumb as they come. Freshman that she was, she hadn't exactly learned her place in the pecking order yet. And despite repeated warnings by wiser seniors, Bree had kept flirting with the best-looking guys at Breton like a cat in heat.

The girl simply wasn't recognizing the reality of hierarchy. Top boys went to Skyler first, and then to her minions who'd earned their position in the Pinnacle Patrol. Of course, outwardly their group is called "Pinnacle Pride", but anyone with two brain cells knows that these senior girls secretly rule the school through a host of soul-crushing maneuvers. At times their efforts might require downright physical strength, which is where their athletic Breton boyfriends often come in. So when Bree Mortimer was spotted brazenly dancing last week at the spring mixer with the boyfriend of Skyler's second girl in command, clearly the little slut had gone too far.

But that's okay. This one was easy.

All Skyler had to do was arrange for Parker's LaCrosse team to walk Bree back to Pinnacle, get her a bit tipsy, and then take turns with her in the Black Woods—that dark grove of trees that separates the two schools, which administrators rarely thought to supervise.

And the best part was, Bree would never say a word.

Oh no—to accuse anyone from the Breton LaCrosse team was well known to be career suicide in Cincinnati. Their fathers head the largest corporations in the tri-state area, and their pockets are deep enough to railroad any poor fool who dares to sully their golden sons' reputations.

"I *said*," Skyler repeats herself, folding her arms impatiently, "did you take care of that little whore?"

"I always take care of business," the voice assures her with an odd, cold finality.

Skyler feels his fingers glide down her arms toward her wrists. She likes to be tied up, to be fiercely pleasured and left gasping for more until her body is shaking and nearly ready to burst. And then she'll do the same to Parker—but her turn will be much harsher, always leaving deep red welts on his back and ass before she screws his ever-loving brains out. Parker wears his wounds like a badge to the LaCrosse team, who envy him like crazy for getting rough, dominatrix sex from the iciest bitch in town.

"You've been a very, *very* bad girl," the voice whispers.

Skyler expects him to crush her breasts between his thick hands now, then slip his fingers down to her sex and grab her violently, throwing her onto the bed where he'll kiss her with such force in so many places that her pleasure teeters upon pain. Afterwards, he'll get off on Skyler whipping him senseless like the derelict he is.

But instead, she feels a rush of wind spin her long, blonde hair around her neck like a soft scarf at first, then harder—more like a noose. Slowly, her hair tightens against her neck until her throat can barely find air.

This is new—

Sex choking?

Skyler had heard of this kinky bedroom game, where the high that follows while your partner screws you and chokes you at the same time is supposed to rival heroin.

But dammit, he should go first. After all, Skyler is pretty certain she can choke the living daylights out of just about anybody.

And knowing Parker, he'd think she's as hot as hell while doing it. Sadistic chicks make the world go 'round, he always said with a smirk.

Skyler feels her hair cinch tighter. She instinctively grasps at her locks to free her windpipe.

"Me first, asshole," she manages to spit out with a hiss.

Parker loves it when she calls him that.

But the squeeze isn't easing up. It's getting tighter—

The hair around her neck is closing so hard it makes her throat burn and stifles any shred of scream.

With her last breath, all Skyler sees are a few, wild forget-me-nots scattered across her journal on top of her dresser, fresh as a newborn day with petals trembling in the cool breeze. As her body slumps to the floor, a ghostly hand rustles through the pages of her pink diary, exposing her secrets. Then it slips off her gold class ring from her finger, the one with PP stamped on it, and holds it over the quivering, candle flame. The ethereal presence presses the searing letters into her forehead like a branding iron before returning the ring to her hand. Picking up Skyler's favorite lipstick, *Rhapsodie en Rouge*, it removes the cap and swiftly scrawls a word across her mirror in the color of blood:

JUSTICE.

2

"Stop it, you motherfucker!"

Creek is standing in our Traveller's wagon in the thin morning light, bare to the waist and slicing his fists through air.

"Stop hurting her!"

One of the TNT Twins' blasts riddles the Turtle Shores Trailer Park with an ear-splitting sound, sending aftershocks through our wagon.

They'd been at it since before dawn, each detonation so loud it echoes inside my molars. Clearly, they must've finished mixing their homemade gunpowder last night, and the boys couldn't wait to have their fun. Any redneck worth his salt will beat the morning sun on opening day of hunting season—or for a damn great explosion.

That's the reason Creek is shadow boxing in his sleep, right? His protective instincts are on overdrive and never rest, even in his dreams. And the TNT Twins' fireballs are enough to set off anyone's adrenaline reflexes...

But I know better.

The shadows that Creek tries to knock down dwell in the deepest recesses of his soul.

We've only been married for a couple of weeks, but Creek's heart is never really mine. Not completely.

There's a chamber inside him that's sealed off, where untold horrors happened in his childhood by the hand of his stepdad—his mother's killer. I hate that man with everything I've got. Because even though he became a fugitive and was never seen again, he's still destroying Creek, bit by bit.

A guy like Creek won't rest till he finds that asshole and erases him from the earth and from ever hurting another vulnerable human being again.

It's both why I love Creek, and hate him sometimes.

Because I can't rest either.

Here I am, huddled in a corner of the wagon with Granny Tinker's soft crazy quilt wrapped around me like a shield, watching this tortured heart, the love of my life, hurl his torment at what haunts him. If I don't get out of the way, he could kill me with just one hook. He whips his fists at the speed of light, his wayward blonde hair dangling into icy blue eyes that never see me, with every muscle in his tight abs rippling in fury.

This is the smoldering dance he does in his sleep at least once a week. I hide in the corner till he gets the hatred out of him and falls, exhausted, back into our bed, but he refuses to talk about it. Whenever he's awake and I try to bring it up, Creek swears he's "fine."

Yet the broken boards inside our wagon stained with blood from his knuckles offer a different story.

Creek throws another punch, and I quietly slip open the latch of our wagon and steal into the cool morning air. The smell of sulphur and smoke engulf me like fumes that have somehow escaped the gates of hell. If it weren't for the TNT Twins' unbridled laughter that fills the morning with their hoots and hollers of victory, I'd be ducking for cover by now. But I'm used to their joyful experiments, the way they leap and do tummy bumps each time one of their spud guns, trebuchets, or explosives work according to plan. As I round the corner, I witness them managing to incinerate a rock. It oozes like lava from an impossible amount of heat, and they give each other a high five.

Good God, what did they get a hold of this time —plutonium?

Then another scent traces along a breeze, rich with the aroma of sizzling bacon, cheese and potatoes, coming from Lorraine's trailer. She, too, gets up as early as the TNT Twins, but for more charitable reasons—she feeds us all her heavenly hash from the scraps of whatever Creek and I can manage to beg, borrow, or steal. It's kind of ironic, I know, considering I have millions stashed away in my father's secret Swiss bank account registered in my name. But he recently put a restriction on it that I couldn't touch the cash till I'm 21. He says the money will ruin me.

Of all people, Doyle McCracken should know. It takes a thief to know a thief, and I'm not about to argue with him.

Why should I? The truth is, I love our life at Turtle Shores, nestled near the banks of Bender Lake, Ohio. Sure, it might look like the boondocks to some people, but the folks here truly love me and have proved it in every way possible. It took an awful lot for me to learn that such love is priceless. I don't mind scraping by for few more years and doing all I can to help out my neighbors. We're a family now here at Turtle Shores—and that's the way I intend to keep it.

If only I could make Creek's heart whole, too.

The smell of Lorraine's cooking draws me like magic to her camouflaged Airstream—a beat-up, old trailer that's so hidden by leaves and brush you have to know your landmarks really well to find it. Nearby, I'm not surprised to find Brandi, Bixby and Granny Tinker sitting in the early morning light on tree stumps and old rockers, snapping Lorraine's green beans. Something tells me they couldn't sleep either, and the scent of Lorraine's cooking is enough to give anybody the courage to venture outside, even if they are intimidated by the TNT Twins' blasts.

Granny casts back and forth on her chipped rocker, her wavy gray hair tumbling to her shoulders and crowned with a black top hat and peacock feather. It matches her long, black dress, which on anyone else would make you think she was about to attend a funeral. But I swear her ruby buttons flare when I come near her, and so does her crystal ball that she has beside her on a lawn chair, as if it has a personality of its own and deserves a seat. Lately, she's been calling it Annabelle Lee.

"Good mornin' Robin," Lorraine calls out, stepping down from her trailer before I've mentioned to her that I'm here. Lorraine is as blind as a bat, and I always find it unnerving that she knows when I've arrived, although I haven't made a sound. How she manages to cook up a storm without burning down Turtle Shores, I'll never know.

"Well, *good* is up to dispute, Lorraine," Granny Tinker cuts in. The pearl-handled switchblade she uses to clip the ends of the green beans flashes in the light of the early sun. For a moment, I wonder if she intends to do damage to somebody with it. "Here," she says, handing me a coffee cup with liquid so dark it looks like motor oil, "ya might need a sip of joe before ya hear this one, Robin."

I accept the mug from her as she opens a newspaper and folds it back. "This ain't a particularly good day for yer Alma Mater," she remarks. Granny Tinker holds up a black and white photo of Pinnacle, the old boarding school I ran away from, that's featured in the morning news. "Damn shame 'bout another death at that high falutin' school of yours. First there was a mysterious fire at a fundraiser that killed some lady named Drew Ball, and now this."

Startled, I set down the coffee and seize the paper from her. Scanning the article, my mouth drops. "Skyler Worth's death by asphyxiation is currently ruled a suicide," I read aloud, "because there were no fingerprints, signs of forcible entry, or foreign DNA upon her skin or in her room. Nevertheless, the case has investigators baffled, due to Skyler Worth's immense popularity as the president of Pinnacle Pride, along with her other achievements."

"Achievements?" I gasp. "She was the most vicious chick I ever met! She ruled Pinnacle through her secret society with an iron hand, doing Mother Superior's dirty work and more. The only achievement she ever had was destroying nearly every girl who crossed her."

"Now, now," Lorraine clicks her tongue, setting down steaming cornbread on a tree stump beside us, which Bixby wolfs faster than I can count to ten. "Be careful about mentionin' the dead. Their spirits can still roam fer days."

"T'ain't no accident," Granny Tinker grumbles, wiping her switchblade across her dress and holding it up to the sun to inspect its sharpness. Her crystal ball radiates crimson again. "The head of Pinnacle's PTA died of smoke inhalation last month, in a three-alarm fire with no causes or sign of arson, and now this. Cops say Skyler's boyfriend couldn't a killed her, 'cause he was waitin' in the emergency room with a sprained ankle. If'n you ask me, them's haints did in those folks."

Granny Tinker points her switchblade to a fuzzy spot in the newspaper photo beside the school. It's hazy and gray, a bit wider at top, almost like a funnel. Just then, another blast shakes the trailer park with a great swirl of air, rumbling so loud I'm tempted to hit the dirt.

"Cut that out, boys! Enough already—cain't you see you woke us all up?" Brandi hollers in her white-spangled jumpsuit, circa 1970s Elvis. Leave it to Brandi to light up the early morning with a bazillion rhinestones that cast a kaleidoscope of colors around us. She yawns and checks her sparkly watch for the time, looking like she's ready to head out for her shift at the Moo 'N Brew Drive Thru. "Besides, yer stinking smoke's made my coffee taste like rotten eggs." Brandi tosses her coffee on the ground and marches over to the TNT Twins in a huff, her finger wagging, but they pay her no mind. They simply dive for the bushes with their homemade cannon made of PVC pipe, giggling.

"Haints, huh?" muses Lorraine, taking Brandi's spot on a

tree stump and rubbing her chin. "Well good," she nods. "I hope that damn Pinnacle burns to the ground for what it done."

I set the paper on the grass beside me, confused. What would Lorraine know about the goings on at an elite school like Pinnacle, coming from a trailer park by Bender Lake? It didn't make sense—

"Well, burning down t'ain't the same thing as justice," Granny warns, waving her switchblade. "I never met a haint that'll stop before karma gets resolved." She glances at her crystal ball on the lawn chair beside her, nestled in one of her old quilts like a pet. For an instant, an image of a golden orb appears inside it that circles in the shape of a funnel, matching the hue of the rising sun, which I take to be a coincidence of light. Just then, Creek walks up to the big dogwood tree beside Lorraine's trailer, nose in the air, taking a whiff of Lorraine's cooking like one of the Colonel's old hounds. Granny Tinker gazes at her crystal ball and lets out a cackle.

And I swear to god, I hear traces of a soft voice whispering on a breeze.

Beware of ghosts who never rest…

Creek steps up and hands me a bouquet of wild forget-me-nots that are the same color as his vivid blue eyes. Ones that see me now, fully awake in daylight. It's his peace offering, I know, because we both understand full well why I got up before he did. His knuckles look like raw meat, even though I can tell he wiped off the blood. When my eyes meet his, I see the veins in his temples throb.

"Good morning, Mrs. Flynn," he gives me that half-smile that breaks hearts, the one that makes the scar on his cheek inch into the shape of a dagger that points to his eyes of electric blue.

But are we really married? Or did I just tie the knot with the shell of Creek Flynn? There's a whole cavern within him that he's never let me see. How do I know that's not the *real* Creek? How will I *ever* know unless he allows me inside?

"Interesting choice of flowers, boy," Granny Tinker smiles at my bouquet, flashing her gold tooth.

I feel the tingles climb up my spine. Dried forget-me-nots were what we found in the small wooden box that Granny Tinker gave to us on our honeymoon, along with a stack of letters from Creek's mother and a simple silver bracelet with the letter "C" stamped on the clasp for her name: Caroline.

Granny points her switchblade at the blossoms in my hands.

"You know, darlin's, you kin find out the truth and settle that spirit once and fer all. If'n you got the guts," Granny says, nodding at the forget-me-nots. "Or that fancy-dancy boarding school you went to ain't the only thing 'round here that'll stay haunted."

Granny shoots Creek a steely glare.

But Creek isn't looking at her.

He's studying the last morning star that twinkles in a baby-blue patch of sky above us, shrouded between the green branches of the dogwood trees.

And his gaze is about a million miles away.

3

I want to swipe Granny Tinker's crystal ball from the lawn chair right then and there and ask it what the hell she's talking about, because heaven knows Granny will never give me a straight answer. How could what haunts Creek be connected to the recent tragedies at Pinnacle? But I don't get the chance because of a tinny, ringing sound that begins to echo through Turtle Shores. Everyone here knows what that means—it's the warning bell system that tells us when someone's approaching the trailer park that isn't supposed to. Without another word, we all dash for the secret bunkers beneath each of the trailers and wagons that were cleverly dug out at one time by Creek and the TNT Twins.

In thirty seconds flat, I'm huddled in the cinder-block darkness beneath Lorraine's trailer. Creek comes down the stairs holding Lorraine's thin frame in his arms as tenderly as a child, her head resting on his ample shoulder. When he sets her carefully on an old couch, with only a nightlight beside it so we can see, I take her hands in mine and rub them to comfort her. It's the unspoken rule here at Turtles Shores that everybody helps those who can't help themselves, and I can only trust that Brandi hid Creek's younger brother Dooley and my parents in the bunker beneath her trailer at the other side of the park. The Colonel makes us do practice drills to keep up our speed at least once a week, so I have faith that everyone is safe.

But the dead quiet unnerves me. The way we can make Turtle Shores seem like an utterly abandoned trailer park within seconds, as though no one's lived here for decades, always borders on something eerie. It's how we survive.

And like usual, Granny Tinker is the only one who remains above ground because she's the fastest talker within three counties—and spooky as hell. Not many people want to hang around here long after dealing with Granny.

Above us, I can hear a low humming and the creak of Granny's rocker. She's playing it nonchalant, singing an old bluegrass tune while probably trimming green beans until the intruder approaches. Then I hear heavy footsteps—it sounds like a couple of men—and my gaze darts to Creek's. I can tell in his eyes of striking ice-blue, ones that are more suited to an angel than a boy from the backwoods, that he's not a bit worried. With her switchblade and any number of venomous spells, Granny Tinker has always managed to take care of herself.

"Yer ghost ain't here, officers," she calls out in a preemptive strike before they can get a word in.

Predictably, there's a sound of shuffling feet. It's always

hard to know quite what to do with the weird information Granny dishes up.

"What's that, ma'am?" a low voice replies.

The creak of Granny's rocker stops.

"She's long gone, son," Granny sniffs. "You oughtta know that by now. An' the man that killed her, too. Or believe you me," a coarse, metallic sound slices through air, like maybe she's sharpening her switchblade on a stone, "we woulda sent his ass to Jesus a long time ago."

"D-Do you know where he is? The man who killed Caroline, and maybe more girls—"

Granny sighs loudly like they're stupid.

"Not every man in a fancy house is above the law, boy—surely you know that. Trouble with you lot is you don't use yer noggin. Look fer the showiest place in that big bright city a yours and that should tell you somethin'."

"Indian Hill? Near the Pinnacle Boarding School?" one of the officers pipes up.

My face is flames. Hot prickles run along my cheeks, seeping down into my neck. They're talking about *my* old neighborhood, where all the posh families in Cincinnati live. Who do they think's doing these crimes? Is there a connection between the deaths at Pinnacle and Creek's mother?

"Besides," Granny continues, "the paper sez that poor Pinnacle girl committed suicide, and t'other one was an accident. So why you runnin' like chickens with yer heads off 'round here?"

"Ma'am," an officer replies sternly, "I think you know as well as we do that there've been rumors around Bender Lake for years that Caroline Gust, who once attended Pinnacle, was killed here by a Breton alum hiding out as white trash."

"That's right," his partner chimes in. "And it's our job to follow all leads. Even the prospect that the man who murdered Ms. Gust is now a serial killer—and he's back at her school to get more girls. Maybe it's just heresay, but other than the coroner's report of suicide, and an accidental mortality, it's all we have to go on."

I shoot a glance at Creek. *Gust?* I thought Caroline's last name was Flynn, like Creek's. Totally confused, I notice Creek's face has become stone, cut from solid marble, as unreadable as a Greek statue's. It's the aloof way he always appears when he's toughing out hard, perhaps impossible, information. Neither one of us had a clue about Caroline's former history at Pinnacle, or that Creek's stepdad might have come from Breton. How could Granny have kept this information away from us for so long? And more importantly —*why?*

"Ma'am," an officer demands, "when was the last time you actually saw Bradford Helms?

"His name warn't that then, and I guarantee you it t'ain't now. That son o' perdition is as slippery as a snake. He dealt meth on the other side of Bender Lake and so abused Caroline an' everybody else he could find that they felt lower n' dust. When he choked her to death on one of his drug sprees, her boy ran him off rather than kill him right in front of his innocent younger brother—who still loved him, the poor child. But if'n you ask me, once a drug dealer, always a drug dealer. I suspect he's just found somethin' else to sell. Like I said, follow the money trail, and I bet it'll lead you straight to him."

There's a long pause. But I know what's happening—the same thing that takes place every time someone we don't want comes around. For a while they search the grounds, unable to find a single soul or clue to what they're looking for. And then they scratch their heads that a crazy old woman like Granny Tinker manages to live out in the sticks all by herself. Meanwhile, Granny keeps up her rocking with a Cheshire Cat smile, till it dawns on the intruders that they've wasted their time, and they leave.

Sure enough, I hear heavy footsteps plod off and car engines start up, the sound slowly fading as they depart Turtle Shores. When I dare to head upstairs, Creek follows me with Lorraine in his arms. The early sun stings our eyes as we surface from the bunker. But what's different from the trailer park I knew only minutes ago is that my whole world has changed. The ground beneath my sneakers feels the same, but inside I've been shot to hell. Bender Lake isn't just *my* boondocks anymore—a safe haven that I share with Creek and my parents. Now I know that Pinnacle and Breton have had their claws in this place all along. I don't know why, but that makes me feel violated and vulnerable, as if I've been struck by some strange, heat-seeking disease that I thought I'd gotten away from, only to discover that it followed me here. Will I ever shake the stain of that wretched boarding school from my soul?

Creek sets Lorraine down gently in a lawn chair next to Granny's crystal ball. For a moment, I swear I see the hazy outline of Pinnacle's gothic main tower in its core, the black PP flag at the top waving in a breeze.

"G-Granny," I stumble, feeling my throat tighten from

nerves, "y-you never told me," I shift my glance to Creek, who's stiff as a soldier, "you never told *us*, that Caroline once attended Pinnacle. Let alone Creek's stepdad came from Breton—"

Granny halts her rocking and stares me down with the most intimidating glare I've ever witnessed. It doesn't help matters that her eyes look like a timberwolf's, gray on the outside with a pool of fiery gold in the middle. She glances at the bouquet of forget-me-nots that Creek had brought me earlier that morning, already beginning to wilt in the sunlight.

"That's 'cause there's a right time fer everything," she points out, her voice gravel. "You warn't ready to know back then. But you're all growed up Robin, an' so is Creek. An' you kin hear the truth now."

Lorraine in the lawn chair nearby nods her head. "Ya see, we got all kinds here at Bender Lake," she affirms. "Not everyone who wears torn jeans and flannel is as poor as they make out to be."

I feel heat stab my cheeks. I'm rich too, in a way—at least I will be in a couple of years. Yet I run around wearing frayed jeans and a flimsy camisole like a white trash princess.

"I-I guess people can be…complicated," I stammer. I haven't actually got a dime to my name yet. No one here does —but we band together so it won't define us. Glancing at my sneakers with holes in them, I notice the hems of my jeans are caked with Bender Lake mud. "Granny," I muster the courage to ask, "can you tell us how Caroline got here? Was she running from the law, like me?"

Granny sways in her rocker once again, her jaw tight, as if mulling over how much I can take. Beside her, her crystal ball turns dark as night. She presses a button on her switchblade so it snaps back into place and tucks it into her pocket, folding her hands. Her rocker halts and she clears her throat.

"Caroline Gust had been…raped, honey."

I want to check Creek's reaction to this horrifying news, but my gaze is too riveted to Granny's. All at once, she seems much older to me—every line in her face creased like well-worn rawhide—as though the memory of Caroline Gust had put years on her soul.

Lorraine frowns at the mention of Caroline's early days at Bender Lake. "Yep, that poor girl came here in her old Pinnacle uniform, pregnant and destroyed, with bruises all over her." She stares in my direction, though her pale green eyes are as faded as sea glass. "I could see back then, darlin'. Caroline had a lot in common with you—she'd stolen a car and drove as far away from that hell hole school as her wheels would take her."

Instinctively, my hand slips over my mouth to cover my jolt. Granny always said, with her eerie tarot cards as evidence, that history has a way of repeating itself. But even though I'm another Pinnacle refugee, I'd never endured anything as brutal as an assault. Granny eyes me warily, gauging my degree of toughness. I lift my chin to signal I can take more.

"Some things can downright break a person," Granny says. "Make her feel like she's damaged and no good for nothin' no more. I don't think Caroline ever recovered. So a course she was prime for a predator like that damned Bradford Helms. Sure as hell, before you know it, a boy from Breton came to Bender Lake claiming he's gonna take care of her, and he hid her out on the other side of the lake like his secret mistress or somethin'. But he beat her senseless, and her kids, too. He was dealing meth from his trailer to make more money than his fat cat daddy. That son of a bitch."

"You know, business is business to dem Breton boys," Lorraine snarls. "They don't care where the money comes from, so long as they git it."

The sound of their words ring in my ears like a foreign tongue. I shake my head to try and take it all in. Can this outlandish story be for real? Yet I know it is—both Creek and I have learned the hard way that Granny never lies. She just tells a certain vein of truth you might not want to hear. Though my heart's hammering so hard it's difficult to breathe, I seek out Creek's eyes, realizing this news must be hitting him like a landslide. But when I turn my head, the place where Creek had stood is now empty, as though he'd slipped away like a ghost. Scanning the trees and meadow of Turtle Shores, he's nowhere to be found.

Granny pulls out her switchblade from her pocket and presses it into my palm.

"Ya might be needin' this, darlin'," she says, "to cut away them honeysuckle branches on yer way to Bender Lake."

I stare at her pearl-handled knife, baffled.

"Now where the hell does that young man always go to solve his problems?" she barks like I'm a dim wit, waving her hand at me to scoot. "He needs you now, honey. So best git along."

Drawing a deep breath, I do as Granny says. But as soon as I head down the overgrown trail toward Bender Lake, Granny calls out, her solemn words chasing my back.

"Like I said before, Robin—you locate the haint that's

been doin' these crimes, and you jes' might find yer way to Creek's momma's killer."

I cut at honeysuckle canes that block my path so I can see, feeling like her voice is following me.

"And the way to Creek's soul."

4

I've walked to Bender Lake dozens of times, yet it feels strange now, as though it holds far more secrets than I'd ever dreamed. Who was Caroline Gust, really? Is Creek the child of a rape? My stomach twists as I make my way down the brambled path to the shore, holding Granny Tinker's switchblade so tight my knuckles hurt. When I reach the smooth, sandy beach, I realize I'm trembling.

I know why.

It's not just the shocking news of Creek's mother's past. It's the fact that, after all Creek's done for me—helping to find my mother in Italy, risking his life for me more times than I can count—I don't know if I have the power to heal him in return. Is my love enough for the dark void that's in Creek? Or will I always be locked out of that part of his heart that's known so much pain?

I stare across the lake, at the early morning mist still clinging to its shores, its water as smooth as glass. A heron spies me and lifts its great wings to glide across the surface that mirrors its flight. I have no idea where Creek might be, but I believe Granny's right—other than slamming at our wagon in his sleep, Creek always seeks out nature to find solace for his troubles. But he knows this lake far better than I, and if he doesn't want to be found, *he won't be*. After all, this is the backwoods guy who can elude Bob's bloodhounds.

Does that mean he'll try to elude *me*?

With that thought, a mourning dove flutters past my cheek, making me jump.

It lands in the distance on a set of footprints by the shore that disappear into the gentle, lapping waves.

Like someone shook off shoes and went for a swim.

I nod.

Of course Creek would lose himself in the water. Naked, without anything else to define him except the scars and tattoos on his skin. It's the only place he ever goes to be completely himself. "Lake rat" he calls it, but sometimes I think it's something more—as though he becomes a phantom in the water's mist.

The mourning dove utters a lonely cry by the lake and takes wing again, blending into the wisps of fog that hover at the water's edge. One of the bird's white tail feathers falls in a delicate spiral and lands on the water, floating toward the tree shadows. It's like the feather Creek always holds in his hand whenever he prays to the spirit of his mother for guidance. Those same prayers are what Granny Tinker claims brought me to Turtle Shores to help provide for our neighbors. I watch the white feather on the water quiver a little as one of the shadows begins to ripple. A shiver inches down my spine.

"Creek," I call out. "Is that you?"

No reply.

"Creek, it's Robin. I'm here—your *wife*. Where are you?"

I'm not quite sure, but I thought I heard a sigh.

That's it, I decide—I'm going in.

Kicking off my shoes, I tear off my socks and jeans, then slip out of my camisole and underwear and leave them in the bushes. All the while I clutch Granny's switchblade in my hand, which I close with a snap. You never know who you're going to bump into in Bender Lake, even at dawn—something Creek taught me when I first arrived at Turtle Shores.

Closing my eyes for a moment, I tough out the raw shock of cold water on my feet and knees, wading in to my thighs and hyperventilating till it reaches my chest. Damn—the water gives me brain freeze as I submerge. I kick quickly to keep my body moving, heading over to the nearby tree shadows on the lake with several stiff strokes.

Yet the closer I swim to the darkness, the more I feel alone...

In this large body of water, surrounded by giant hardwood trees and dense thickets of honeysuckle and raspberries, I'm as small as that white feather I see swaying on the lazy current.

And inside, I feel as distant from Creek as if I were at the bottom of the ocean.

"Creek," I whisper loudly, "are you here?"

The small cove I've entered merely echoes my yearning voice.

What can I possibly say to him that he'd want to hear?

I'm sorry your mother was assaulted? That your childhood was as bad as they come? There's nothing in my lonely, rich-cage childhood that can compare, no matter how often I withstood my father's lies. Doyle McCracken still loved me, in spite of all his mistakes, and he moved heaven and earth to try and prove that to me.

I spy an inky patch near the lake's edge, its shadow hovering on the water like a stain. I've got a hunch what it is—one of the underwater caves that Bender Lake's famous for, a haven for stolen goods and contraband. It's not unlike those secret chambers in Creek's heart: murky, dark, and impossible to enter. As I dog paddle in place, feeling the cold water slip over my skin like silk, it hits me. Maybe this mystery is part of what I fell in love with in Creek. Brooding, distant, and dangerous as all get out—yet so passionate about love when he really feels it. The boys at Breton were always showy and obvious, flashing their sparkling smiles and designer sneakers. I wanted something different. But now I realize Creek is as remote as the dark side of the moon.

And I can't escape how isolated I feel. Because that darkness dwells in my heart, too.

"Creek," I call, exasperated. "I *know* you're here. I can feel it…"

It's true. Something makes my heart skip whenever his presence is nearby. And right now my heart's doing flip flops.

"You can't fool me, Creek—I know about these caves. You showed them to me, remember? The secret places you hide and come up for air. Whether you like it or not, I'm with you, right there in the dark. In my heart. Isn't it time we turn the light on? No matter what it exposes, at least we'll really see each other—"

Another ripple glides through the water, fluid and silent as a snake. It heads into the inkiest shadows laced by threads of mist near the shore.

"I don't know…"

Creek's low voice echoes over the lake. It fades slowly away, as if it were made of mist.

I take a deep breath, my arms and legs still treading to keep myself afloat.

"I do," I reply defiantly.

My throat chokes up for a second. I clench my teeth and will it to stop.

"You told me when the gypsies married us in Italy that you gave me your heart," I remind him sharply. "But you lied, Creek. You're just like my dad. 'Cause part of your heart belongs to your mom's killer, whether you want to admit it or not. He's the real shadow that comes between us. He *controls* you, Creek. Makes you shut yourself off from even the one who loves you most."

That got him—

I see Creek's wet blond hair surface, those crystal blue eyes of fractured ice arresting me as though I've pierced his soul. His stare becomes angry blue flames.

And he disappears.

Dammit!

I can't take another minute of his fucking invisibility act.

But in seconds, I realize I couldn't be more wrong—

Fingers clench hard around my wrists as stiff as handcuffs, and he's *anything* but invisible right now.

"*No one* controls me!" Creek seethes.

All at once, he's staring me in the face. His hair drips over his sharp cheekbones like a newly-born Adonis. Yet the water around us seems to warm with his anger in a funnel of underground heat. He clutches my wrists tighter, and I wince from his iron grip.

"Ouch!" I cry, breathless, feeling the welts rise on my skin.

Nevertheless, I glare straight into his eyes.

"Oh?" I spit out, trying to wriggle away, only to feel his fingers burn. "Then how come you're hurting me right now? Who's voice are you listening to—'cause it sure as hell ain't mine!"

Creek doesn't flinch while my eyes drop to the *Partners* scar I once carved into his bicep. It's healed now but red and throbbing, like a beating heart—his heart.

I click Granny's switchblade in my hand, flashing its sharp, wet edge.

"I swear to God, Creek," I hiss furiously, "I'll plunge this knife right into that scar if you don't let go of me! I'll cross out *Partners* for all time—"

That's when I see him wince—ever so slightly. Not over the possibility of pain. He's tough as nails, and I know he couldn't care less about bodily harm. It's because he can tell I mean it. I'm ready to walk away for good. Screw the *Partners* idea—that whole crazy marriage thing—unless he starts getting real with me.

Creek's gaze shifts to the gold wedding ring on my finger, the one he got from the Travellers, that's dripping a trail of cold water down my clenched fist. In a motion so swift he frightens me, he whips Granny's switchblade from my hand. His lip curls into that dagger-scar smile that scares the crap out of most everybody. But then he tenderly traces the knife edge along my cheek, pressing it into the outline of a heart.

"C-Creek," my voice trembles, not sure if he intends to slice the knife into my skin. He can be a crazy motherfucker sometimes, and every muscle I have tenses as I steel myself for the worst. "We can't ever be *Partners* of the heart as long as that asshole who killed your mom stands between us. You gotta heal this thing—or you lose *me*. You promised, Creek, when we came home from Venice."

In his darkening eyes I see a bottomless pit of pain. This is a guy who withstood childhood horrors most caseworkers have never even seen. The same guy who discovered he could've been fathered by a rapist. And this is the man I love so much who's afraid that there's something in him that can never, *ever* heal...

Just for a moment, I actually feel his grip tremble a little.

Then Creek releases me and slips under the water again, taking the switchblade with him.

He completely disappears, leaving me in the shadows of the lake.

As far as I'm concerned, he might as well have stabbed that switchblade straight into my heart.

Maybe this is it for me, I realize. Alone in a vast body of water in the dark. Forever reaching for Creek's heart, only to grasp at shadows.

Maybe all men lie, like my dad. They tell you what you want to hear for a little while, then make you carry their baggage for the rest of your days. What was I thinking? Creek's a seasoned criminal. Shadowy, elusive—and always with the upper hand. What made me think he'd ever crack open his full heart to *me*?

But then I hear a swish of water. And after that, a voice in the darkness…

"Okay."

The sound echoes along the surface of the water and floats toward me like a spirit.

Soon, a warm breath hesitates against my neck. Startled, I feel his lips press upon my wet skin, absorbing me as if he could syphon away my soul. Before I know it, I'm enveloped in Creek's arms. His sinewy legs clasp around me like a vise—as though he owns me, and I'm caged inside his strength. He slides his palm down my arm, his fingers clutching my hand over my gold wedding ring.

"This water is where I first touched you," he whispers, soft as a thief and sending goose bumps over my flesh. "Where I first breathed onto your skin—"

He swivels me around to face him, treading his legs and cupping my cheeks in his hands. "This lake is as big as my heart, Robin," he confesses. "You're mine, *my wife*, and I'm never letting you go. You think there's something between you and me—but you're wrong. We're like this water."

He raises his hands high as if in prayer and lets the water trickle over my forehead, where it flows and collects on my lashes. Blinking, I draw a deep breath and dare to gaze into his eyes.

"There's no place where we don't touch," Creek insists, stretching his arm wide over the lake and watching the water drop from his fingers like it's a part of him. "We're *are* this infinity."

He glances up at the sky, at the streaks of gold that thread across the morning like our tangled hopes. "I'll make sure of that, Robin."

I'm choking up again, treasuring this feeling of our skin on skin, my breasts pressed against his hard chest in this big old lake that's as deep as his impossible-to-fathom heart. And despite my best efforts to hold them back, tears slip down my cheeks and return to the lake. I grit my teeth, hoping Creek won't notice, but the way he's looking at me right now—I can tell there's no lie in this man. His liquid blue eyes are all intensity, all focus, as if I'm the only thing that can give him breath. Yet I also know there's a ragged road ahead that we have to follow down together, or else it will become the very hammer that breaks us apart. I lean my forehead tenderly against Creek's, and work up the courage to say it.

"Creek, does that mean you'll go with me to find out what's happening at Pinnacle? And the *truth* about your mom? 'Cause Granny says it will lead us to her killer."

With my words, the motion of Creek's legs that have been gently treading to keep us afloat stops. Strangely, he allows us to submerge, pulling me deeper and deeper, till the lake water's so dark I can't see him anymore. My heart begins to race, and in a panic I try to wriggle away, wondering if he intends for both of us to die here. Just when I'm running out of breath, he kisses me so hard, like it's the last thing he'll ever do, and yanks me up to the fresh air. Gasping desperately, I feel him stretch himself out to float on the water and drag my body on top of his like a second skin. We are one with the mist now that collects over us like dew.

"Robin," Creek whispers, "if I go with you to Pinnacle, we might not come back the same people we are now."

He is quiet for a long while, and all I can hear is the sound of his breathing and the call of a mourning dove somewhere in the canopy of trees. Its soft coos are so haunting that I feel a shiver pass over me as we gently sway on the water. Creek threads his fingers through the ropes of my wet hair, stroking me tenderly as if he's afraid I might break. "Robin," he fractures his silence, "we might be changed forever."

"I know," I reply, feeling the droplets of mist settle cold upon my skin. "But we'll be together. *Really* together. And isn't that all that matters?"

With my heart in my throat, I can feel Creek's chest muscles tense up as we float on the lake, seemingly towards dawn. Slowly, a soft golden sheen from the sun strokes our naked bodies and warms us a little.

Creek nuzzles his face against my neck as his hand strokes my hair. "Yes, Mrs. Flynn," he finally whispers, giving me a kiss. "That's all that really matters."

5

We huddle together in our wagon beneath Granny Tinker's quilts, still a bit damp after putting on our sandy clothes that we retrieved from the bushes near Bender Lake. In front of us on the bed is the weathered box Granny gave us on our honeymoon—the one with Caroline Gust's old letters. Hesitantly, I creak open the dark, wooden lid, feeling as if I'm about to peer into our future as well as her past. The candles I've lit in our wagon spread a warm light inside the box that's lined with red velvet, sparkling off my mother's heirloom ruby heart on a silver chain that was once shot to pieces by Creek. The Stone of Thieves—he didn't want a damn thing to do with its magic anymore, or the havoc it wreaks in people's lives. As I open the lid wider, I spy the star-like cracks where Granny Tinker glued the ruby shards back together, and the sight of that mysterious stone makes my breath catch. It doesn't help matters that the flickering candles in our wagon cast shadows that dance like gypsies around a bonfire, only making me more anxious. Swallowing hard, I pick up Caroline's faded bundle of letters held together by twine. When I glance up at Creek, I detect a wince.

Her handwriting. Her thoughts. Her soul inscribed on these tattered pages...

It makes me feel like I'm holding Caroline's heart.

Creek has never read his mother's words. Never knew they existed before receiving this box, or gotten a glimpse into why she endured such unspeakable things at the hand of Bradford Helms. His jaw twists as my fingers unravel the knot over her letters, letting the twine fall to my lap. The pages in my hands are yellow and oddly curled at the corners, though they've been lying flat in this box for years, fastened in a bundle. And there are peculiar little puncture marks in the center of the pages as if an animal held them by the teeth or claws. That thought sends shivers down my back, and I wonder if one of Granny Tinker's familiars somehow collected Caroline Gust's writings for her to store in this vintage box for posterity. Did her crystal ball tell her we might one day be brave enough to read them? Just as I ponder the possibilities, I hear a mourning dove call outside.

And inside the box, the Stone of Thieves flashes crimson...

"C-Creek," I stammer, totally spooked by the red glow pulsing from the ruby right now, "I know why you didn't kill your stepdad in front of Dooley, after all he'd been through. You didn't want to scar him with the sight of violence like that after losing your mom. But why didn't you go after the guy later?"

Creek's fists clench till his knuckles crease white. His eyes become glacier-cold, gazing at the ruby heart as if he could freeze fire.

"I *did*," he seethes.

There's a rage coming from Creek that practically sparks off his skin, all at once making me feel far too warm beneath our blanket. His eyes never leave the ruby heart as he clears his throat.

"That's why I became homeless, Robin," he confesses in a voice of coarse gravel. "I criss-crossed the country for six months, hitchhiked from Canada to Mexico and back, stole cars, drove everywhere. It's why I started a life of crime and moved Dooley to Turtles Shores, where Brandi and Granny Tinker volunteered to take care of him out of the goodness of their hearts. But that asshole skipped the country, and his trail evaporated."

"The-the ghost at Pinnacle," I stutter, "it could be Caroline's ghost—she'd know where he is, right? What name he's using now?"

The heat from the ruby heart in the box rivals Creek's, making my forehead sweat.

"These letters," I lift them to Creek, "we can hold them while we grasp the stone to find out what happened. Just like we did to locate my mom. If we touch something personal of Caroline's and the ruby heart at the same time, the magic might—"

Creek's jaw slices across his molars like a crosscut saw. The anger coming from him in waves severs the words in my throat.

"But then we'd see her again."

Creek's response leaves me breathless.

It's only then that I appreciate the depth of his pain. He was raised by a woman who became a drug addict, abused by a monster, yet who allowed her children to be harmed as well. I know my dad wasn't nearly as bad, but my mother was just as devastated by circumstances and practically catatonic when we found her.

"My mom was a victim too," I pipe up tenderly. "You saw how she was in Italy and what her dad had done to her, how he crushed her soul and locked her away in a convent."

I dare to touch Creek's arm at his *Partners* scar. He flinches away, his skin hot. Nevertheless, I stand my ground.

"Your mom was abused, too, Creek. You heard Granny— she was raped. Whatever she allowed to happen, you gotta realize she was broken and forgive her. That guy—he wasn't just some white-trash trailer park addict. He came from Breton. I know these types, the way they sell drugs to compete the easy way with their daddy's big-time money. They're ruthless! What was he dealing, anyway?"

"Crack. Meth, You name it," Creeks spits out like a fire.

"And what did he call himself? I mean, when you knew him?"

Creek turns away.

"It doesn't matter."

"Maybe it does," I say gently, reaching for his shoulder again. "Maybe if we say his name aloud it will help the ruby heart to find—"

The second I touch Creek's skin, he's up in an explosion, throwing things and tearing at our wagon. Shoes, boots, books, a teakettle and a mirror fly—crashing against the curved slats of wood. I've never seen him like this, not even in his sleepwalking rages. The veins are nearly bursting at his temples and his biceps bulge, quivering with power. He's a whirlwind of anger, breaking cups and saucers with each name he spits out.

"Buddy! B.B.! Bill!" Creek fumes. "Don't you get it? His name was different every month. *HE* was different every month. He sat us down and made us call him something new to avoid the cops while he sealed the deal with these."

Creek points to the rows of scars from cigarette burns and knife cuts on his arms that he'd covered with tattoos to keep people from asking questions. "These wounds meant we'd better keep our mouths shut about the truth—and about him."

Creek glares at me, his eyes as cold as someone who learned how not to feel pain a long time ago. And I realize in horror that even the scar on his cheek that turns into a dagger whenever he smiles was carved by someone he hates more than anyone in this world.

No wonder, in the entire time I've known Creek, I've never once seen him glance into a mirror…

"His wounds are all over your heart," I whisper, more to myself than to Creek. I grab Granny Tinker's switchblade that he'd brought back from the lake and hold it up to his face. The pearl handle shines in the candlelight.

"Do it, Creek," I demand. "Write the name that matters most between us: *Partners*."

I roll up my sleeve and click the switchblade open, pointing the knife over a candle flame.

"I want to hurt like you do. I'm in this forever," I insist.

Creek's eyes grow wide. He looks at me like I've lost my mind.

"Then I'll do it myself," I promise. Before Creek can say a word, I slice the knife edge into my skin, drawing blood.

"No!" Creek cries, grabbing me. He wrestles the switchblade easily from my fist and tosses it across our wagon, where it lands against a mirror fragment with a crash. Smoothing my damp hair from my face, he gazes into my eyes.

"You're *perfect*, Robin," he says with eyes a softer, liquid blue then I've seen in ages. "I-I don't want to you become like *me*. Damaged. Haunted…"

"But we're one heart," I remind him. "And as long as *you* bleed, so do I."

Creek kisses me—the kind of kiss that swallows me like water. His mouth presses so hard, as if he hopes to somehow fuse with my being, and I can taste the slight flavor of iron from the blood on his lips. When he breaks away, his eyes are all concern—and warning.

"Robin," he says, glancing at the ruby heart that still glows in the box, "I'll go along with the magic of the stone one last time. But only if it can keep you as beautiful and perfect as you are now. Not broken and bewildered, like my mom—"

"But that's not the point of love," I cut in. "Surely Granny's told you that. Love is supposed to be all rough at the edges. Two souls who collide and explode and leave their pieces all over the place to rub against each other and get messy and tangled in one another. Love hurts sometimes, Creek. That's how I know you loved your mom so much— because of the pain you're in. It's not smooth and perfect like

Bender Lake at dawn. Or like the sterile life I had back in a rich suburb of Cincinnati."

I gaze about the wreckage of our wagon, each shard of the broken mirror reflecting my own face back to me. "Love is chaos, like this," I observe, smiling at Creek a little. "But at least it's real. And I want, more than anything, for our love to be *real.*"

Creek stands with his fists still clenched. Every muscle in his body is as tight as the strings on a violin, though there's no threat inside this wagon but my open heart that wants him to heal. I notice there's blood dripping from his knuckles. Before he can stop me, I swipe some on my finger and take a lick.

He grabs my wrist, as if he fears it might have some voodoo affect on me, and I brush what remains of his own blood on his palm like paint.

"Martiya, my ancestor, used to rub people's blood on their hands to tell their fortunes," I remind him. Wriggling my arm free, I lift the ruby heart from the box and wipe some blood on the cracks of the stone. "Let's see if the Stone of Thieves will show us the way, Creek. Take one," I hold up a letter of Caroline's. "I don't care if you get blood on it. Take it and read it out loud."

Creek is a solid pillar of granite. Not a single one of his muscles loosens. Yet I know he admires my guts—it's what made him fall in love with me. Finally, he clears his throat a little, and I see his eyes fill with that protective instinct that would kill anyone—anything—that tries to mess with me.

"Robin," he says gravely, "what if we get trapped inside the stone, like you did the last time? There's no rhyme or reason to its magic—"

"Then at least we'll be together," I reply.

Creek's cheek scar slips into that dagger smile. He loves my sense of adventure—maybe even my recklessness. "That's my girl," he says slyly, tousling my hair.

Creek takes Caroline's letter from my hand and holds it up, his thumb staining the old paper with his crimson fingerprint. In the candlelight, I can see her words in ink through the back of the page, with a rounded, immature script like she was only a teenager, perhaps, when she wrote it. But after scanning a few lines, Creek's face grows troubled, as though what he reads is much darker than her age would indicate. He motions for me to sit down with him on the bed.

Nodding, Creek holds the letter for me to read too. "She led a tough life at Pinnacle, baby. Just like you," he sighs.

I draw in a deep breath and place the ruby heart between us, so we can both hold the stone while he reads aloud. My heart's hammering, because I don't know if we'll be transported in a vision to whatever Caroline was going through—or if we'll be trapped inside the stone for all time. Either way, I'm prepared for whatever I have to face with Creek. Rubbing my finger along the star-like cracks of the stone, filled with Creek's blood, I feel the ruby grow hot and throb beneath my hand.

And for the first time ever, I hear Creek's voice break as he reads Caroline's difficult words aloud.

❧ 6 ❧

Dear Bright Eyes,

I write these things to keep from killing myself.

I know that's a lot to put on somebody. But you're the only one I feel safe talking to.

You've kept my secrets ever since Grammy died, never interrupting me no matter how many times I cried. God knows, you can't ever leave a part of your soul laid bare when the PP are around. That stands for Pinnacle Pride, by the way. Or Pinnacle Patrol, as everybody calls them. They're the senior girls who rule our school. They know my grandma passed away of a heart attack a month ago, and now they think I'm open season.

This bracelet with my initial on it is all I have left of her. Grammy was the janitor here at Pinnacle. The PP made fun of me all the time that my only guardian cleaned toilets. "Shit Maid" they called her, and they heckled both of us whenever they could. But Grammy only wanted the best for me. She saved for years to give me this bracelet from Tiffany's so I'd feel special. It doesn't compare to the diamonds the other girls have, even on their custom-made, designer backpacks. But it means the whole world to me.

Now she's gone. And I have to face my senior year all alone without her protection.

You see, Grammy saw something.

She never told me exactly what it was, because she didn't want the administration coming after me. It had to do with one of the Board of Directors' behavior toward another girl. One day, when I was starting my junior year in a public school ("hillbilly high" everyone at Pinnacle called it, because most of the folks in our white trash neighborhood came from the boondocks), Grammy sat me down and said I'd be switching to the new school where she worked. I'd live in the dorms, just like the other girls, with a full scholarship. Grammy never lied to me. She said this was all a form of "hush money." As long as we didn't talk, I'd get the finest education Cincinnati has to offer. "Act like you know their secrets, darlin'," she warned, "and believe me, they'll be leavin' you the hell alone."

They left that other girl alone, too. Grammy made sure of that. She was one tough bird, but gentle in her own way. Kind of like you, Bright Eyes. The day you came to my window after her funeral, I almost felt like it was her. You have the same gray coloring and soft eyes, and the way you sing reminds me of her gentle voice. I'm giving you these letters to take away so the PP can't dig through my stuff and find them. I trust you'll fly them somewhere safe, hopefully somewhere beautiful. Maybe to a boondocks place, like Stone Cross Creek, where me and Grammy used to live when I was little, before we moved to the city. The only home that ever made me feel free.

And though it kills me, I'm giving you my bracelet, too. All the girls are thieves here. They have everything they could ever want, but it's never enough to fill them up inside. And they know exactly what to steal to destroy your soul. Sometimes, in kinder moments, I figure they must want other people to hurt as much as they do. But in weaker moods, I swear to God I wish they were dead. Or I was dead. Anything to keep them far, far away from me. Maybe someday, when I graduate and I'm old enough to be free of this place, you can take me to where you've hidden the bracelet and my letters. You, my only friend. But for right now, I have to protect myself and not let the PP get under my skin.

Thanks for listening, Bright Eyes.

Oh, and one more thing before I go.

Today, I got a little glimmer of hope.

The kind of hope that I don't want the other girls to know about and try to rob from me.

It's just a feeling. I'm not really sure. But I might have made a new friend.

He's a guy I met tonight at the spring dance at Breton.

Tall and beautiful. Lanky as a leopard. With a deep voice that reminds me of a purr as he moves in shadows.

And the way he looks at me. Well, it was like I was made of sunrise.

For just one moment, standing in front of him in a party dress that Grammy got for me at the Goodwill, I felt like maybe this life could be worth living after all.

Honest to God, he was a fresh, new breeze that blew into my heart.

And everyone says he's crazy.

— CAROLINE

I hear a voice continue after Creek finished the last words of Caroline's letter, echoing in our wagon like a ghost. But Creek's lips aren't moving.

"They don't own you," the voice insists.

To my astonishment, we aren't gazing at the letter in Creek's hand anymore. We aren't even *inside* the wagon.

We're staring at a tall young man with long, brown hair, streaked with warm, honey-colored strands. He has on a navy blazer adorned with the gold Breton insignia and faded, torn jeans. His soulful blue eyes, the same crystalline color as Creek's, are fixed upon us as if…

As if…

We're *one* person.

I glance around, but I can't find Creek. All I can perceive is what Caroline saw in that very moment—this drop-dead gorgeous guy from Breton—as though I'm trapped inside the memories of her soul. Panicked, I want to scream, to thrash and break away from the confines of Caroline's spirit, till I feel Creek's hand clutch mine, though I can't see him. It's then I realize that we're both inside Caroline somehow, locked within her memories, watching her life unfold when she was a teenager as if these moments had never really passed. They still exist somewhere, in a parallel dimension that maybe only the Stone of Thieves can access. The warmth and strength of Creek's hand wrapped around mine encourages me that we'll be okay—at least we're together. And maybe, when the ruby heart is finished showing us what it wants us to understand, we'll be free…

"*Nobody* owns your soul," the good-looking guy from Breton repeats to Caroline.

It's dark out, and he's leaning with a devil-may-care attitude against a wall in the Breton high school hallway, his arms crossed under the amber corridor lights. Slowly, he recedes into the shadows as a flock of Pinnacle girls come around the corner, giggling and twirling to show off their sleek party dresses. One of them spots him in the darkness, and their chatter halts. She edges aside and tugs at her friends' elbows to give him a wide berth, as if he might be dangerous.

"Watch out ladies," the guy whispers from the shadows. Barely visible, his lips crease into a half-smile that reminds me of Creek. "Or I'll slip through your windows at night…and show you what crazy *really* means—"

He lunges after them with the quickness of a cat, spooking the girls and sending them into a panic, their high heels clacking down the hall. One of the girls loses her shoe in the shuffle, and it makes the guy laugh. He emerges from the shadows and picks it up, looking it over before handing it to Caroline. Inside, the label on the instep says *Valentino*.

"Hold on to this. You never know—you might become a princess at midnight," the guy smirks. "Sherwood," he gives her an overly formal bow like some troubadour, spinning his hand with a flourish before he stretches it out to greet her. "Sherwood Flynn. Renegade artist and occasional truant."

"Caro—"

"I know. You're Caroline Gust."

He smiles as if he harbors a secret and shakes her hand. Yet his intense, almost feline gaze absorbs her completely, not like she's the granddaughter of a simple janitor—more like a star who's lit from within. "Everybody around here knows who you are. You're the most beautiful girl at Pinnacle. And that, Caroline, is why they hate you."

His eyes fall to the shoe in Caroline's hand, which glitters under the amber light like a constellation.

"You're a ward of Pinnacle, huh? Just like me at Breton." He tilts his head a bit, searching her face as though solving a riddle before smiling again. "Along with being bat-shit crazy."

Now we can see Caroline, too. Her large green eyes and winsome face are framed with pale, wavy strands of hair like Creek's. And her willowy frame in a plain, ivory dress makes her glow beneath the amber lights like some ethereal heroine from an old, black and white movie. She blushes as much at Sherwood's gaze as his words, nervously pressing her hands over her satin dress as if she's self-conscious about where it came from. Or perhaps because he called her crazy.

Sherwood grasps the shoe from her hand and holds it up in a mock toast, giving her a wink.

"Here's to free spirits," he smiles. He glances at the halls of Breton, at its heavy sandstone exterior flanked by occasional gargoyles. "May we one day find our wings—"

"W-What makes you think I'm...crazy?" Caroline interrupts, her voice testy yet hesitant as she gazes at the sparkling shoe in his hand. She swallows hard, taking a step back before daring to stare him in the eye. "If anything, *you're* winning the weirdo contest. Scaring girls from shadows? Bowing to me like you're a...I dunno...a dandy or something? Don't you think that's a little gallant?"

Sherwood shakes his head and sighs, his eyes darkening.

He presses the shoe back into her hand before grasping her shoulders.

"This is what real gallantry is, Caroline," he replies, his voice low and tense. "Protecting those who can't protect themselves. I don't believe for a second you're crazy. And neither does Pinnacle. But they're going to do everything in their power to prove you *are* so you can't be a threat anymore. You got signed up for Wednesday afternoon therapy sessions with Dr. Cutler, right? Ever since your grandma died? I saw you waiting for him in Memorial Hall. Kids from Breton and Pinnacle both see the same guy."

He shakes her a little in his urgency, glaring into her eyes. "Now repeat after me: They don't own my soul."

Caroline's eyes grow wide. She bites her lip and shakes her head slowly. "They don't," she affirms. But then she straightens her back and throws off Sherwood's hands. "And neither do *you*. Or the PP," she hisses. "Fuck you all—"

Sherwood eyes sparkle. He claps his hands together, beaming with pride. "That's the spirit!" He gives her a fist bump. "But if you think me or those bitches at Pinnacle can mind game you, Dr. Cutler's far worse," he continues. "The guy's a tool for Pinnacle. He's gonna try to plant an idea in your head that your grandma never saw anything. She was just some nutty old bat. And anything she told you is fiction, 'cause you're her relative and crazy too, get it? Oh sure, he sounded real nice and listened to you for a while at first, didn't he? Understood your loss and pain?"

Caroline's gaze shoots to her pale, second-hand pumps that are a little scuffed at the edges, searching the ground for a moment. Her eyes well with tears from memories of her grandmother that are still too raw. "Yeah," she nods.

"That's his con. And I bet he gave you a prescription to 'improve your moods,' right? But they're really designed to make you a zombie. A perfect Pinnacle geisha mannequin who'll *never* talk out of turn—"

"I haven't taken them yet," Caroline cuts in angrily, glaring into his eyes. "Who the hell are you, anyway? How dare you say this shit to me?"

She breaks away from him and begins marching toward the parking lot with determined strides.

Sherwood leaps to her side and spins her around. Caroline tries to take a swing at him with the sparkling shoe, but he catches her by the wrists and holds firm.

"Dammit, Caroline—you don't have the time you think you have," he warns. "If you don't act the part, they're going to get you committed. Do you hear me? Don't take those pills, but behave like you do. In Dr. Cutler's sessions anyway. And whatever lies he gives you about what your grandma did or didn't see, repeat them to everyone in authority like a puppet. Or you're going to be spending your days in a padded cell. If you don't believe me, ask yourself what happened to Julie Givens once your grandma died, and why she disappeared from school last Friday. She's another scholarship kid like you, the one that man from the Board hit on."

Tears slip down Caroline's cheeks as she wriggles free and takes several steps back from Sherwood, trembling.

"H-how do you know about Julie? And what my grandmother saw?" Caroline's words burst from her lips way too loud, nearly a screech. She covers her mouth with her fingers, frightened by the rawness of her own voice.

"They *talked* about you, about what happened, in Memorial Hall. Dr. Cutler and an administrator from Pinnacle after your session. I learned to put my ear to the heat registers a long time ago. They're practically like telephones. Knowledge is fucking power around here."

Caroline closes her eyes for a moment, as if it were all too much to take in. Then she lifts her gaze to search the stone gargoyles that cast eerie shadows into the Breton halls.

"It's okay," Sherwood says compassionately. "I know the ways to beat their game and avoid the worst before you graduate. So you can get out with your sanity intact. Unless you really *are* crazy, like me?" He smiles.

"So what are you in for?" Caroline asks.

"Being an artist, full throttle. Wild at heart. Apparently that's a crime around here. Oh yeah, and skipping class and running away. Worst of all, seeing my mom shove my dad over a yacht—that got me thrown into psychiatric lockdown. When I was released, she sent me away to be a ward of Breton till I turn eighteen."

"Oh my god, your dad drowned?" Caroline gasps, reaching for her lips. "I'm so sorry—"

"It's okay," Sherwood shrugs. "He was a prick."

"I'm sorry about that, too," Caroline says.

"Look, you gotta get back to the front parking lot." Sherwood points down the hall. "And catch the van to Pinnacle with your chaperone before it leaves. Or they'll notice you're tardy and keep a closer eye on you. And that's exactly what we're gonna change."

"What's that?"

"Pinnacle and Breton knowing a damn thing about what we do."

Sherwood flashes a smile, the kind that can sweep most girls' hearts away, just as a mourning dove flies past him and lands on a gargoyle. Its haunting coos distract him for a second before he returns his gaze to Caroline.

"'Cause from now on, Miss Caroline Gust," he says, slipping back into the shadows and giving her another embellished bow, "you gotta friend in crazy."

The ruby heart pulses vibrantly in my hand. When I turn, I'm startled to see Creek beside me again. We're still in the wagon, released for now from the Stone of Thieves' spell. As relieved as I am to be home, my fingers grip the ruby heart too tight with worry.

Was this guy—this Sherwood Flynn—Creek's *father*? And Caroline's molester? It's hard for me to image Caroline taking the guy's last name of Flynn for her son if he'd assaulted her. I stare at Creek, unable to deny the resemblance between them. They both have the same tall, agile frame and cockiness in their eyes. Yet that crystal blue of their gaze can freeze you in place sometimes, when the mood strikes. Creek has that expression right now—he stares at me so coldly I can hardly breathe.

"Robin," he says quietly, the hard angles of his face reflected in the crimson glow of the stone. "We shouldn't go any farther."

"Why?" I protest. "We're getting to the heart of what happened to your mom—"

"That's just it. She's still innocent. What happens next she might not recover from. I don't want you to see something that could break your spirit—"

"Mr. Creek Flynn," I cut him off sharply, setting my palm on his powerful thigh. "I'll have you know I'm a hell of lot tougher than you think. Only a while back, I was locked in a dungeon in Venice and beaten by thugs, and I survived just fine. Remember? Okay, so you rescued me. But I think I can take whatever we're about to see. And the real question is," I gaze into his eyes defiantly, refusing to be cowed by his icy stare, "can *you?* Can you watch what happens to your own mom without your anger trapping you in the stone, like it did to my ancestor Martiya? Forever marinating in hatred—"

"I'm *not* Martiya," Creek seethes.

Despite his protests, his fists twist our bedsheets into knots.

"Oh?" I remark, tapping one of his clenched hands.

"Watch me," he replies, surprising me by stealing a hard, impulsive kiss. Something in the bold way his lips overpower mine says he's got this—and he's not about to let anything come between us. Not even his own rage. He hugs me tightly afterwards, cocooning me inside his warm, strong arms, where I feel his heartbeat pounding on my chest as if it were my own. This is a guy at war, on the front lines of a battle I don't completely understand, but ready to do whatever it takes. When he breaks free, he looks into my eyes as if they hold a key to his future—*our* future. There's a bond between us that's seen us through bank robberies, corrupt relatives, even death threats. This bond is so strong it can take us through hell and back, if Creek has anything to do with it.

"We can make it through this fire," Creek whispers to me. The hair on the back of my neck stands on end. He runs his fingers gently across my forehead to sweep a wayward lock of hair from my eyes, then cups my face in his hands to swipe another kiss.

"Believe in me, Robin," he says, staring at me with such intensity that I swear he could burn a hole into my soul.

"I-I do," I stutter, still blown away sometimes by the force of Creek's fierce love for me. He's the only guy on planet Earth whose gaze can leave me reeling.

"Then are you ready to do this again?" he asks tenderly. "No matter what we have to witness?"

"Yeah," I nod, clutching his hand as if it's my security blanket.

Creek exhales a long, slow breath and grabs another one of Caroline's letters from inside the old box. He holds up the tattered, punctured page to the flickering candlelight, where I can see her handwriting through the glow like a set of encryptions—a secret road map to her heart. Giving my hand a squeeze, Creek begins to read her letter aloud...

Dear Bright Eyes,

Tonight I tasted what it's like to fly.

"Taste" is a funny word, I know. But seriously, it tasted like straw and corn husks and country dirt, all thrown together in a blender with a touch of spring wind.

I guess it's a long story.

And I've never been so scared in my whole life.

But it was the best day EVER.
So here goes…

All at once, we see Caroline's memories again as if they were happening in real time. We're inside Caroline's dorm room at Pinnacle as the sun is beginning to set, creating long tree shadows that extend like fingers over her sparse furnishings. Caroline appears to be studying a history book at her desk, her finger toying with the rim of the sparkly, high-heeled shoe she'd kept from the other night like a memento. Her reading is interrupted by the odd sound of heavy breathing, followed by a few groans. When she glances up from her book, she spots Sherwood crawling through her window. He lands in a heap on her floor, laughing.

"I'd bow for you again, Miss Gust," he smiles mischievously. "But I'm afraid I'm a bit…indisposed." He struggles awkwardly to unfold his long legs.

Caroline drops her book, stifling a scream. But then, in spite of her shock, she bursts into giggles, blushing. She dashes over to Sherwood and hoists him beneath the arms to help lug him to his feet.

Standing up, Sherwood brushes off a few leaves from his button-down Breton shirt and unravels a twig from his messy, shoulder-length hair.

"What the hell are you doing here?" Caroline gasps in a restrained whisper, so the hall monitors won't hear.

"Well my friend," Sherwood gives her a cocky grin, "I trust your roommate is still on sick leave with mono? You must be awfully bored in this crummy room all alone—"

"How the hell do you know she's gone?" Caroline replies. "You've been *stalking* me?"

Sherwood rolls his eyes and points at the heat register on the floor.

"Oh yeah," Caroline chews her lip. "You heard me mention that to Dr. Cutler in my session, huh? Well you'd better watch out, or I'm going to listen in on *your* therapy appointments, too."

"That's okay," Sherwood grins. "I'm an open book of crazy."

At that moment, a dove lands on Caroline's windowsill, accompanied by a rush of cool air that flings the curtain open wide.

"Feel that?" Sherwood smiles. "A strange cold front seeping into a warm, spring evening?" He folds his hands behind his head and nods. "It's calling to us."

"What is?"

"Adventure. The elements. The basis of everything that's art. Earth, wind, fire—and risk."

All at once, Sherwood's eyes are ablaze. He edges toward the window and holds out his hand, doing an abbreviated version of one of his bows. "C'mon, Caroline. Let me show you my world. It's pure poetry."

"Sneak out? Are you kidding me?" Caroline stares at his palm like it's something forbidden, maybe poisonous. "What if we get caught? It's not like I have room and board waiting for me somewhere if I get kicked out of here—"

"We *won't* get caught. We won't even be late for last check at lights out." Sherwood nods toward the wall clock that says 7:30. "The night's still young Caroline."

Boldly, he steps over to her bed and creates a lumpy form beneath her sheets with pillows, tossing the bedspread over it. "It's high time you expanded your horizons. See?"

Another burst of cool air rushes through the window and swirls into the room.

"It's inviting us. Let's take a break from this place. Consider it a little—vacation. To preserve our sanity."

Caroline rolls her eyes and shakes her head in disbelief.

"You know, they're right, aren't they?" she says. "Everybody claims you're nuts. You ace all your classes without attending half the time, and you create wild, abstract paintings, but you don't let anyone know how you do it." She pauses for a second, her eyes narrowing. "You're not the only one who can listen behind closed doors," she notes, lifting her chin. "Some of the teachers call you a brilliant delinquent. Destined for the correctional system. Others say you're a genius who's gonna be famous. Which one are you?"

"Do I have to fit into a category?" Sherwood asks. "Let me fill you in on a little secret. I just happen to listen to my muse when the mood strikes. That's all."

Another gust of wind penetrates the room, rifling Sherwood's hair. He nods as if hearing its urgent whispers. Then he glances at Caroline with eager, tender eyes. "Will you come with me?" he asks. "This once? I swear you don't ever have to do it again. But I promise you, what you're about to see will make your soul fly."

He stretches out his hand once more. Nervous, Caroline checks the clock on the wall. She hears the wind whistle through her window, almost like a summons.

The cold breeze whirls just enough through her room to

rustle homework pages, lifting them into the air and making her shiver.

Caroline stands, her arms wrapped around herself, staring at the window as if she's at a crossroads. She gazes around her dreary room for a moment, then at Sherwood, as though carefully weighing what each one has to offer.

"Your grandma's not here anymore," Sherwood mentions softly, gazing at a picture Caroline has of the woman with her mop and janitor bucket in an old frame on the desk. Her face appears warm but stern, wearied by hard work. "No one's in your corner, Caroline. Who you decide to be depends on *you* now. Are you going to stay that frightened girl in a uniform with her hands folded who always does as she's told?" He points at a medicine tray on her dresser filled with small orange pills. "Who they can control with a prescription? Or are you going to start winging it a little and dare to lead your own life?"

Caroline glares at him, her hands descending to her hips. The breeze lifts her hair now too, as if tantalizing her.

"You know, you look really beautiful when your hair's a bit wild."

"Where are we going?" Caroline demands, crossing her arms.

"I don't know," Sherwood answers. "Honest, I don't. Where the wind blows—that's the only thing for certain. But when we come back, I'll give you one of my paintings. As long as you don't tell anybody how I make them."

Caroline gazes at her sterile room, devoid of any color, style, and certainly any art, as though her life—her very personality—has already been prescribed for her along with her tray of pills. She glances up at the relentlessly ticking clock that looks as though it came from an institutional catalog. For all she knows, it could have hung in a hospital room before ending up here.

"Okay," she whispers, as much to herself as to Sherwood. "But you'd damn well better get me back here by lights out at ten, or I'll claim you kidnapped me. *You're* the one going to juvenile hall—"

"Miss Caroline," Sherwood smiles slyly. "Believe me, it would be entirely my pleasure to serve time for kidnapping the likes of you."

"Don't you *dare* bow to me again, either," she hisses.

Sherwood laughs, his lips sliding into that half-smile again. "As you wish," he replies.

He grabs Caroline's hand and escorts her out the window, into the mottled, warm colors of the setting sun that filter through the trees. Together, they scale down a flimsy metal ladder that leans against the side of Pinnacle's ivy-covered stone walls. When they reach the bottom, Sherwood folds the ladder and dashes with Caroline behind a tall hedge, where he'd hidden a rusty VW Bug, the color of a robin's egg, with enormous wheels. He tosses the ladder into the trunk and shuts it quietly, only to glance up and see Caroline with her hands to her face.

"What the hell? Where'd you get this car?" She glances around anxiously.

In spite of her nerves, Sherwood hops into the front seat and starts the engine. He leans out the passenger side window and smiles at her. "I'm not stealing it—I'm just borrowing it for the sake of art," he replies. "How else did you think I was gonna bust you out of here?"

He opens the door and waves for her to get in.

"We'll give it back," he assures her. "Just with a few more miles on it. Hurry up—we don't have time to waste!"

Caroline wrings her hands, then straightens the pleats of her uniform skirt, running her fingers along the sharp creases.

She gazes piercingly into Sherwood's eyes, as though measuring his trustworthiness. The wind picks up again, blowing her long, blond hair into a tangle past her eyes.

"This is it, Caroline," Sherwood says. He releases the parking brake and lets the car roll forward a little. "Who you gonna be?" His tone has become far more serious, yanking at her attention. "Who Pinnacle tells you to be? Crazy and alone? Or are you gonna come with me and see something new? 'Cause until you take the wheel, Caroline, you'll never really be in control of your life."

Caroline quickly glances to either side of the street to see if anyone happens to be watching. But the hedge is so high it obscures the car completely from nearby Pinnacle windows.

"All right," she relents, walking around to the driver's side of the car. She opens the door and gives Sherwood a hefty shove from behind the wheel. "But *I* drive."

❧ 8 ❧

"**J**esus Christ! You didn't tell me you don't know how to steer a car!" Sherwood hollers, his eyes as big as saucers.

"That's not true. I drove my grandma's Buick all the time. It's just that it was an automatic, and this—"

"Is a souped-up Baja Bug with a bazillion horsepower. What did you think? I was gonna borrow a piece of shit? You can give me the wheel any time, you know—"

"No!" Caroline insists. "I hardly know you, Sherwood. If I'm not allowing Pinnacle to control my life, then I won't let you, either."

"Touché," Sherwood smirks as they continue down a backcountry lane about thirty miles south of Cincinnati. "C'mon, let's go stare beauty in the face. If you've got the guts."

Sherwood's enthusiastic gaze is infectious, even to Caroline in the glow of the dashboard as the sky becomes darker at the brink of twilight. After glancing his way, she stubbornly reserves her eyes for the dirt road ahead of them to keep from getting distracted.

"What kind of beauty can you see in the dark, anyway?" Caroline spits out. Her fingers grip the wheel so tightly her knuckles press white.

Sherwood rolls down his window. A burst of oddly warm, moist air fills the car, so different from the cool breeze that kept penetrating her dorm room, almost as if they'd driven past a sauna.

"Feel that? That's Kentucky air duking it out in spring. Hot versus cold, and loaded with as much force as an atom bomb."

"And that's a *good* thing?" Caroline blurts, her brows crinkling together.

Just then, a hurl of wind rocks the car so hard it's difficult for Caroline to manage keeping the VW on the road. She snakes left and right before gaining control again, when all of a sudden, corn stalks from nearby farms fly across the road like javelins.

"Holy shit!" Caroline cries. She ducks as they whip against the windshield, fearing it might shatter. "We're caught in a storm!"

"Not caught," replies Sherwood with a lopsided grin, curling his knees and settling his sneakers on the dashboard. "Chasing it, my dear."

"What??"

Caroline immediately pulls to the side of the road and cranks on the radio. Up ahead, they see a string of lights in procession, similar to a parade, from vehicles parked in an enormous irrigation ditch. Over the radio, the announcer says in a thick southern accent that there are tornado warnings in a broad swath across northern Kentucky, affecting mainly rural areas and horse farms. No touchdowns have been recorded yet, but they could happen any minute.

"Christ, we've gotta go back!" Caroline panics, grabbing Sherwood's arm and jiggling him.

"Not at all," he replies calmly. "Storms are like life, Caroline. You either run away from them or toward them. It's your choice. And right now, we're heading straight for the eye—"

"Oh my god—we've got to warn those people!" Caroline points to the lights of the cars up ahead. "They must not be aware—"

"Oh, they're aware all right," Sherwood nods. "In fact, they're our competition."

He squints, surveying the darkening twilight and the swollen, curtain of clouds that press down upon them like a gray blanket. "But time's on our side."

"N-No it's not!" Caroline stutters, desperately scanning the horizon for a funnel. "The radio said a tornado could happen right now!"

"Yep," Sherwood replies. "So you'd better park in that big ditch, or we'll be on our way to Oz."

"How about gunning it instead?" Caroline counters, wild eyed. "And getting the hell out of here!"

She steps on the gas and cranks the wheel, spinning the VW in a tight u-turn that throws up billows of dust, when suddenly she spies a funnel in the distance, advancing toward them.

"Too late!" Sherwood notes, grabbing the wheel and

steering the VW into the deep irrigation channel, large enough to swallow the car.

Without even glancing at Sherwood, Caroline hits the brake and bolts free from the vehicle to dive for the dirt, surrounded by a thick embankment. She throws her hands over her head, the way she's probably been taught since grade school.

Sherwood calmly reaches into the backseat of the car to grab several cans of house paint and a large canvas that he tucks under his arm. He joins Caroline in the ditch and crouches, only to lay down his materials. Then, to her surprise, he returns to the car to fetch more. When he approaches her again, he's carrying a thick mallet and iron stakes. He lays down beside her, protecting her with his body as well as his canvas, as one by one the other cars and vans leave, tearing down the country lane like demons escaping hell. When Caroline glances up at the vehicles, she notices they have logos of local TV stations.

"At least they've got a lick of sense!" she shouts to Sherwood, her voice competing with the noise of the wind.

"News crews," he adds. "But they're not leaving because of self-preservation. They're taking off because it's too dark. They can't get a good shot anymore."

"Shot? Of what?"

"The funnel, silly," Sherwood replies. "Good video footage of a bonafide twister can haul in a fortune," he smiles.

"Then what the hell are *we* still doing here?" Caroline digs in her pocket for the car keys, till Sherwood grabs her hand.

"We're painting with the finger of God," he replies seriously. He points to a barn in the distance with an outside light that illuminates a swirl of corn stalks spinning furiously into the sky, with dirt erupting on the farmland, tossing debris everywhere. In the glow of the barn lamp, the funnel appears to heave in and out as it gains strength, almost as though it's a living, breathing creature.

"Okay, get in the car and drive *now*, if you want to go!" Sherwood hollers. Eyes electric, he grabs his canvas and mallet and tucks them under his arm. Then he picks up his stakes and cans of paint. "I'll meet you back at school!" He stands up and waves her on. "I'm going to capture something the videos can't! You won't believe it when you see it!"

"No!" Caroline rises to her feet and clutches his shirt. "You'll die out there!"

But her words are swallowed by the oncoming twister's roar, louder than a jet engine. Oddly, it's a combination of many tones at once—some are high and whistling, others undulating, like a deep, baritone choir singing. And then, at the base of its rumble, is a sound that rivals a heavy freight train, shaking the earth.

"Go! Go!" Sherwood appears to cry out, pointing at the dirt road.

But Caroline can't hear him any more. She can only see his lips mouth the words as he waves her on before he dashes, like a madman, straight into the corn field.

And right into the path of the oncoming twister.

The funnel whips planks from the barn roof into an angry swirl, pausing to toss fence posts and outbuildings into the air as easily as a blender. It heaves in and out for a moment, as though considering its next victims, then surges erratically forward.

Petrified, Caroline watches Sherwood hammering down his canvas and rolling heavy boulders onto it, his long hair lashing at his face. Quickly, he tips paint cans over the canvas and begins to back away as the funnel grows closer, pursuing him like a dark finger in the field. Caroline can't bear it any longer, and she screams before getting up and dashing after him. Shreds of corn stalks and dirt fill her mouth and nose. Leaves and wood chips whip against her face. Nevertheless, she reaches Sherwood and grabs his arm.

"You have to come! NOW! While you still have a chance!"

"No, go back!" Sherwood cries. "Drive away! I've gotta see what happens!"

"I'm *not* leaving you here!" Caroline shouts stubbornly.

All at once, she sees a multi-colored glow at the base of the oncoming funnel, reflecting the last hints of sunset like tongues of fire. In the center, the colors swirl and converge into a ruby eye, pulsing as if its the funnel's heart.

Just like the Stone of Thieves…

Caroline turns Sherwood's shoulders to show him, before linking her elbow in his and dragging him against his will toward the ditch. Despite her determined strides, the wind picks up both of them, causing them to fly for several yards as though a bomb had gone off, while Sherwood's paints explode into a rising spray from the force of the funnel that lifts the canvas into its maw.

And at that moment, everything goes black.

9

Creek and I gasp for breath inside our wagon, feeling like we've been thrown by the twister, too. How do we interpret total darkness? Sherwood and Caroline *couldn't* have died—Creek's living proof of their togetherness beyond that moment, right?

Squeezing the Stone of Thieves harder in my hand, I crease my eyes tight and try to force myself to see more details of their memories. But the only thing I can detect is that the ruby heart has become cold. Creek's palm is wrapped over mine, and I glance at our overlapping fingers, realizing that the stone is no longer glowing. It's murky and heavier than ever. What's more, when I pick up the stack of letters from the old box, they seem like dead words on the pages now. It's as though we've lost Caroline entirely, her voice and her memories, along with the vibrancy that was inside the ruby.

Creek gazes into my eyes with a look I've never quite seen before. It's a cool resignation, like he knows he's been trumped somehow, and is far too smart to fight against fate. He clears his throat and stands from the bed. Grasping my hand and giving it a gentle yank, he helps me rise to my feet.

"It's time to go see Granny Tinker," he say cryptically.

My mind is a whirl.

Can he be serious? He wants to actually approach Granny for *help?*

Such a move is a double-edged sword. I can tell from Creek's gaze he knows that. Granny's as likely to fill your head with her spooky brand of southern-fried riddles as she is to give any useful guidance. And no matter what she says, it will gnaw at your soul for days. Dealing with her is like falling down a rabbit hole. You never know what effect she'll have, or whether you'll still feel like *you* by the time you leave.

Nevertheless, as I turn the ruby heart over in my hand, it feels like a cold rock. There's no magic here any longer. And if we want to find out more about what happened to Caroline, we're going to have to rely on another source.

"Okay," I nod to Creek, drawing in a deep breath. "Let's see what Granny has to say."

We step out of our wagon into the bright sunshine, and I realize it's been months since I've dared to venture to Granny's place. The first time I met her, she seemed like an eccentric witch from some strange fairy tale, yet she turned out to know far more about me than I understood about myself. As Creek and I meander down the slim, twisting trail, no wider than a deer path, lined with a tangle of buckthorn bushes that tear at our clothes, I shake my head a little. No one ever seems to find Granny in these backwoods unless they want it bad enough. Or unless fate decides they need her peculiar wisdom.

Up ahead, in the shadows of an ancient-looking oak tree surrounded by scraggly vines, I spot Granny Tinker's wagon. It's decorated with faded, yet beautiful red and gold scroll designs, and has antique shutters over the windows with small moons and stars carved into them. Yet the mud on the large wagon wheels appears fresh, as if maybe Granny travels at night when no one's looking. With that thought, I spy hoof prints in the soil—but I've never once seen a horse at Turtle Shores. And part of me wonders if Granny somehow changes into a steed under a full moon. The idea gives me goosebumps.

All at once, I feel a splat against my cheek. I taste something sweet, yet mildly tart, dripping onto my lips. Another splat-splat pelts my forehead and hair, accompanied by the sound of giggling. Creek turns to me with a lopsided grin, a runny trail of red slipping down his jaw, the color of blood. He points to a raspberry bush that's noticeably wiggling.

"Dooley," he calls out, squinting. "I can see you. And you too, Granny."

Sure enough, out pop Granny and Dooley, Creek's six-year-old little brother with ivory hair, just like him. In their hands are tell-tale wooden slingshots with eerie figures that look like wizards or shamans whittled into them. Dooley is grinning from ear to ear. He defiantly reloads several raspberries into his weapon and aims it at Creek.

"Forgiveness," Granny Tinker calls out in a commanding tone. She raises her slingshot high like a royal scepter. I half-expect she wants us to bow.

"No way," Creek replies, laughing. "Game on!"

In a flash, he dashes to Dooley and grabs him by the overalls. Turning the boy over, he gives him a shake before snatching the berries from his hand. They two begin a full-on raspberry war, splatting so much red juice on each other and the ground that the area soon looks like a crime scene. I quickly decide my only hope is to duck behind Granny's wagon. To my surprise, I find her already standing there, her arms folded and smoking one of her slim cigars.

As soon a I join her, her husky cackle fills the forest. It always amazes me that she manages to wear her fancy top hat, long velvet gown, and crimson lace-up boots, even for a berry fight.

"Forgiveness, huh?" I rib her, laughing. "You didn't really think we'd let your ambush slide without a return attack?"

Granny doesn't even give me a sideways glance. She nods at her crystal ball that's sitting a few feet from her wagon, nestled in an old quilt on a distressed rocker. Slowly, the chair begins to swing on its own, which disturbs the ever-living crap out of me. Then her crystal ball becomes hazy, appearing to fill with smoke.

Granny slides her cigar to the corner of her lips, clenching it tight between her molars and flashing her gold front tooth.

"That ain't the kinda forgiveness I was referrin' to," she says ominously. In spite of Creek's and Dooley's shrieks of laughter, Granny's face appears solemn. "To tell ya the truth, it's somethin' I wrestle with myself sometimes. Ain't it, Annabelle Lee?"

She nods at her crystal ball. In that moment, the smoke inside it begins to swirl. It transforms into a funnel that makes my heart race, like seeing Caroline and Sherwood chase that twister again. When Creek ducks behind the wagon and joins us to avoid Dooley's berry aim, he catches the apprehension in my eyes. He spots the crystal ball in the rocker, and the sight of the funnel stops him cold. Granny smiles at Creek as though he arrived right on time.

"You gotta forgive yer ma, boy," she says in that voice that's part rasp and part penetrating to your heart's core. "Little bit by little bit. If you wanna see each piece of her life."

She puffs on her cigar and blows a lazy stream of smoke, watching it disappear into the air around us like a ghost.

"It don't come all at once," she sighs. "Kind of like breathing. One breath at a time is how you git along. See, I know a little about what yer goin' through, how sometimes the person you love most can seem to turn on you and become somebody you don't know."

Her eyes narrow, and for the life of me, I thought I saw the image of Pinnacle rise up from her crystal ball. Its gothic spires emerge from the smoke, threaded with wisps of mist, when I spy a figure in one of its windows. Honest to God, it looks to me like Mother Superior—

"You kin be as close as I am right now and not know a person at t'all. Till you crawl inside their heart." She puffs on her cigar some more, watching the smoke overtake her crystal ball again. Her rocker stops swinging.

Creek appears as mesmerized by the creepy ball as I am. Swallowing hard, I finger the cold Stone of Thieves inside my jeans pocket.

"But we tried," I burst a little too fast. I gave up attempting to be subtle with Granny a long time ago. "We read some of Caroline's letters aloud from that old box while holding onto the ruby heart. For a while we could see her life at Pinnacle. But then the visions—or whatever you want to call them —stopped."

"Then somethin's blocking you," Granny replies matter of factly.

"What?" Creek asks.

I've never seen him question Granny Tinker in any way. He usually waits for her to come around and drop her spooky thought bombs on us in her own time and in her own way. And though his eyes are an intense, acid blue, I can tell he's every bit as nervous to find out what happened to his mother as I am.

But Granny Tinker just laughs.

The maid enters Swan Hall at Pinnacle, an elegant ballroom that features white paneling with gilded accents and an ornate swan chandelier decorated with hundreds of twinkling lights. She carries a tray of orange-cranberry scones to serve those attending the annual Spring Mother-Daughter Tea. Using engraved silver tongs to gently place a scone on each attendee's china plate without making a clink, she ignores Gwynn Sterling in the back corner of the room who is not-so-subtly berating her daughter before the guest speaker arrives to give the address. In spite of Gwynn's harsh words, the maid steps over to drop a couple of scones on her plate, then smiles and floats to the others in the room, appearing to be used to it.

"Why *aren't* you a member of Pinnacle Pride yet?" Gwynn scolds her daughter Claret, knowing she only has a few minutes before the program begins. She scans the room with envy at the other girls in uniform who are seated closer in the audience to Mother Superior, almost like her wingmen. "You're every bit as smart and beautiful as they are. What's been going wrong? We shouldn't be seated here in the back. You're a total embarrassment to me."

"I-I told you a million times," Claret responds in a shaky voice, appearing close to tears. "They're brutal. They tell me I'm fat, and ugly, and I'll never be part of their group unless—"

"Unless *what?*" Gwynn demands, crossing her arms.

Claret chews her lip. "Unless I-I bully the other girls," she whispers.

One of the seniors seated next to Mother Superior stretches taller in her chair, turning to to nod with a haughty look in Claret's direction. Claret nods back, her eyes full of fear, as though anxious about what might happen to her if she doesn't.

"Dammit," Gwynn reprimands. "This school is a stepping stone for your whole life. Everything that happens for you next —the right college, the right job, the right fiancé—is a direct result of how you perform now. And let me tell you, it costs a pretty penny."

She jiggles Claret's arm to make sure she's listening.

"Hear me? Don't blow it! Do whatever those girls tell you and get in their inner circle, no matter what."

Gwynn's eyes flash fiercely as she holds up her PP ring and taps it. "You only have one more year left to get your ducks in order. Or you're going to wind up like that pathetic Caroline Gust, who went to Pinnacle with me years ago. She threw away all her chances on some crazy boy and never stepped in line like we told her to, even after we took her to the Black Woods and made things clear. Last time I heard, she died alone and broke in some trailer park. So I want you to go sit down next to their ringleader right now and behave like she's your new best friend. I don't care if you don't really like her— act as if it's your job. Because my dear, it *is*."

"B-but they—they wanted me to lock a freshman girl in the basement all night. There are rats in there, and feces. And somebody said it's haunted—"

"They do it to toughen her up!" Gwynn explodes, swiveling her daughter around. "Look at those girls next to Mother Superior. They're calm, cool, and unflappable. A bomb could go off and they'd still keep their affairs in order. Here," Gwynn grabs a scone from her plate and takes a bite, then hands it to Claret, "put some food in your belly and get your game face on. And don't you dare whine to me again until those girls are your best friends—"

Gwynn's voice is cut off by a sharp wail that pierces the air.

At the sound of the siren, everyone in the audience glances up to a horrific sight in the sky. A dark funnel in the distance is advancing for the school, spinning tree limbs and sign posts into its gray vortex, devoid of light, despite the bright sunshine outside.

"To the basement! Now!" Mother Superior rises to her feet and commands, gesturing at her senior girls to usher the others as fast as possible to the stairwell. Gwynn and Claret stand in shock for a moment. But then Claret does as her mother told her—she runs after the most popular senior girl at Pinnacle to help her guide attendees downstairs.

Still holding her china plate, however, Gwynn doesn't budge.

She's too busy pounding at her chest with her free hand. Her mouth works like a desperate fish, attempting to expel the piece of scone that got caught in her windpipe when she gasped at the sight of the twister. Gwynn reaches for a chair in the hope of flinging her body over it to perform a self-inflicted Heimlich maneuver, when the glass panes on the tall ballroom windows explode from the force of wind that's so strong it topples chairs. Gwynn's hair whips furiously at her face, and she dashes toward the door to try and get someone to help.

Yet strangely, when she reaches the entrance of the ballroom, the door slams shut. Despite her frenzied efforts to open it, the knob appears to be locked. Gwynn falls to the floor, her face nearly blue now for lack of air. Eyes wide open and unblinking, she stares at the sparkling shards of glass in the ballroom, only to see the swan chandelier swing violently and come crashing down.

Gwynn's mouth finally falls slack. A ghostly hand carefully wriggles the gold PP ring from her finger. It sets the ring gently upon her tongue before assembling shards of glass on the floor into the form of a word:

BITCH.

10

After eating Lorraine's fried catfish lunch that she whipped up for everyone in the trailer park, Creek had slipped away from the group quietly, the way he often does when he needs space to mull over difficult questions. I find him high on a tree stand in the late afternoon, one of many that serve as sentinels for Turtle Shores. This particular stand is his favorite because of its beautiful view of the sunsets over Bender Lake. He's sitting cross-legged on the wooden platform with a newspaper spread over his lap. As I make it up the last rung of the ladder and sit down across from him, curling my knees and leaning forward on my elbows, he glances at me with eyes that register that strange new resignation of his. He hands me the paper and gazes across the lake, as though its smooth surface might reflect back to him some kind of understanding.

"Another Death Strikes the Pinnacle Boarding School for

Girls," I read the headline aloud. My heart punches into my throat and my pulse quickens. Scanning the article, it talks about how a mother's death at the school was apparently due to an accidental choking. Yet her gold PP ring was found in her mouth along with the word *Bitch* written in glass pieces on the floor. There were no witnesses or fingerprints discovered on any of the shards. The occurrence is so bizarre it has all of Cincinnati talking about the haunted happenings at the school. What's more, now Pinnacle has brought in an exorcist to help "cleanse" its halls, yet enrollment continues to drop at an alarming rate.

When I set the paper down, Creek's staring at me with that hyper-intense focus of his that can unnerve just about anybody. Like Granny, he has a way of making you feel as if he can see into every nook and cranny of your soul.

I swallow a deep breath and dare to offer up a theory.

"I think Caroline's ghost must be doing this," I tell him, shaking my head. "For some reason she's furious at Pinnacle— or at whatever happened to her there. Or maybe that's the last place she actually felt good about herself, before she started her slide, so she won't let go—"

"We need to get the Indian," Creek sighs, nodding.

Granny I can understand. Her advice might be mysterious, but it usually hides some kernel of truth. I'm not sure about some Indian—or if I can take another backwoods spooky type.

"C'mon," Creek says, "let's go."

He digs into his pocket and holds up a rusted key. It has a face etched on it, the kind you see on the back of a buffalo nickel. It dawns on me he's talking about his old motorcycle.

"W-Where are we headed?"

Creek stands up and gives me a lift. He stares into my eyes like he's worried about me, but also like his back is against a wall. For a long time he says nothing—just gazes at me as though soaking me in. To my surprise, he kisses me softly as if he wants to hold this moment—and maybe hold my heart— just as it is, before something in his life can corrupt it. When his lips leave mine, he whispers into my ear.

"We're heading to the past."

He reaches into my jeans pocket and pulls out the Stone of Thieves. It's so dark and cold now it looks burnt. "To the heart of the black hole that was my life. Where my mother died. To see what it has to tell us."

This doesn't make sense to me—Creek wants to return to his family's old trailer, where Caroline was murdered? Why wouldn't he go to Pinnacle first, where her ghost seems to be? But since this is the only time Creek's ever offered to show me where he grew up. I'm willing to follow his gut instinct. Perhaps facing the darkness of his childhood will offer the breakthrough we need.

After scaling down the tree ladder, Creek takes me by the hand to a set of bushes where he hides the vintage Indian motorcycle he restored. It still has a tractor seat and lots of odd spare parts that keep it together, and I shudder as I recall that this was our getaway vehicle for robbing our first bank. As ugly as it looks, it can go from zero to a hundred in a flash. And when Creek starts it up, it sounds like a raging dragon that could swallow Turtle Shores whole, emitting enough smoke to make me hack. Nevertheless, after he climbs on, I sit directly behind him, wrapping my arms around his chest and squeezing with all my might. This won't simply be a journey around the lake—it will be a pilgrimage for us to the site of everything horrible Creek ever experienced, and I can't help but tremble in the warm, afternoon sun. Creek lurches forward with the bike, and before long, the wind is whipping my hair against my face. I tuck my cheek onto Creek's shoulder and say a brief prayer.

Oh God, I whisper, *no matter what we find, please help Creek heal. Help him bury the past and those ghosts for good, so he can be whole. So we can be whole…*

In spite of my nerves, though, I have to admit the ride around Bender Lake is beautiful. The water sparkles in the dipping sun as we take gravel backroads that rim the shore, sometimes startling ducks and herons into flight. We wind along narrow dirt paths around the lake, shadowed by thick green hardwood trees, heading into what I can only guess is a "holler"—a deep area of woods where no one else seems to dwell. Finally, we approach a thicket of bushes mysteriously threaded with crisscross lines of barbed wire. It's shadowy and has a dark, foreboding feel. Sure enough, I see a glint of chrome beneath some tall bushes—the evidence of a trailer that's disguised like the ones at Turtle Shores.

As Creek brings the Indian to a halt and turns off the engine, he slips off the bike and warns me not to step into any of the nearby puddles. Upon closer inspection, I realize they have sharp stakes peeking through the surface of their water. Razor wire loops in unexpected places through tree limbs and around shrubs leading to the top of the trailer. And there are rusty-looking canisters randomly sticking up through the grass that I suspect are some kind of improvised explosive devices. The whole area is overgrown and desolate—as if no one's been around here in years.

Cautiously, I take a step towards the trailer, but Creek's hand stops me.

"Wait," he barks. Picking up a large rock, he throws it hard at the trailer and then grabs me by the waist, hitting the dirt. It's then that I feel the gun that's tucked into the waistband of his jeans.

The rock strikes the trailer with a thud, and nothing happens. I'm shaking, stunned that Creek's stepdad is so dangerous he feels he has to take these kinds of precautions before entering their old home. What was Creek expecting—a firestorm of bullets? Breathing hard, I stand up when Creek does, eyeing the trailer warily.

"Meth dealers shoot first and ask questions later, unless they're expecting you," Creek explains. He motions for me to stay behind him as we advance toward the trailer. Creek brushes away the shrubbery and uncovers the rusted trailer door. "Get down," he whispers.

I do as he says and watch him swing open the door as fast as lightning.

And fire—

Twice.

At each end of the trailer before I can blink.

The sound of his gunshots rattles me to my bones.

"Trailer's empty," Creek nods.

I have no idea how he knows that, because when he pulls

me to my feet and I peer inside, it's as dark as deep space. But I suppose if no one's left groaning from a gunshot wound, then it's abandoned.

Still, I forget to breathe.

Creek actually thought he had to shoot before entering this god-forsaken place?

I'm not sure what's scarier—the fact that whoever lived in this trailer is *that* dangerous, or the fact that Creek once called him "stepdad."

I suck in a deep breath, trying to wrap my head around the realities of Creek's childhood.

Creek steps in before me, pulling back dusty curtains to let in light. What I see in the harsh sun's glare is overwhelming—a disaster of a place littered with broken meth pipes, old lighters and empty zip lock bags. And there are strange swaths of burn marks across the floor and racing up the walls. Creek sets the Stone of Thieves down on the cracked and yellowed dining room table.

It's glowing.

"The ruby heart wants us to be here, Robin," Creek says solemnly, nodding at the stone. "I had a hunch that's why it grew cold in the wagon. When we arrived here, I could feel it warming in my pocket. There's something we need to find."

He runs his fingers beneath the moldy couch cushions and turns them over in swift, routine fashion, doing the same with rugs on the floor. His face is oddly detached, as if he's totally accustomed to the way things used to be hidden here. After throwing over a couple of mattresses in the back, he finally turns his attention to an old recliner that's faded and threadbare. Tossing aside the cushion, he swivels it around and turns the bulky chair upside down. There, on the bottom, is a blue, stuffed bunny with stains on it along with a little notebook. Both items are secured to the chair with duct tape. Creek peels them off carefully and glances at me. At the top of the notebook is the name "Caroline" written with crayon in a child's hand.

The look on Creek's face breaks my heart.

The way his jaw works back and forth tells me he must have written that word as a little boy. Probably to impress the mother he loved.

He hands the notebook to me with a world of pain in his eyes, clutching the stuffed rabbit to his chest.

Yet the ruby heart radiates so brightly, it appears as if it could melt through the table.

Trembling a little, I dare to open the green composition book, the kind you get in grade school, that's become faded and a bit frayed at the edges with what look like baby teeth marks. The first few pages are stuck together with gum, and several of the early pages have candy-colored stains or have been ripped and crumpled. But then I notice most of the sheets are filled with loopy crayon letters that repeat over and over, in different colors, the way you do when you're practicing your ABCs. It's so dear for me to see evidence of Creek as a child, as someone young and innocent, since I've only known the hardened guy who was forced to be a provider by the time he hit his teens. At the bottom of each page is a big pink heart and the words *Good job, Creek! I love you!!*

Tears come to my eyes as I scan all of the smiley faces, suns, and words of encouragement that Caroline had written. It's only when I peer farther into the notebook that I find an entry that seems to be by her. There's only one, and it's written on a separate scrap of paper smeared with blood that had been folded and jammed into the notebook. The page is stiff and brownish now. Sucking up my courage, I glance up at Creek, then dare to read Caroline's words aloud:

Dear Bright Eyes,

I doubt you'll find me here. Something tells me not even you, my best friend, could locate me in the depths of hell. But I'm not leaving. Not without my babies. I'll fight to the bitter end for my babies.

Bradford locks the door and sets explosives around the trailer so we can't get out. I tried to file a restraining order against him once. I snuck out and grabbed the boys, but he found us and chained us to the table for days. Dooley's the child of one of his "customers" that left him behind after a drug spree. I couldn't let that precious child go back to them. They never even noticed he was missing. They're like zombies, Bright Eyes. All they ever do is feed their habit and destroy everything in their path. And Brad's become crazy. He thinks he owns us, but he's wrong. Every time I try to fight him, though, he grabs me and injects me with something that leaves me knocked out for days. He's worse than Dr. Cutler ever dreamed. When I do finally come around, I discover the scars he's left behind on me and my precious angels. He's a monster, Bright Eyes. He only lets us out at night, and I homeschool the boys when he's not looking so they'll know there's something more to this world. Something more than their mommy could give them.

Why did I ever believe he loved me? At first life with him was wonderful. Bradford said I was his sunshine, and he'd give me a new start after what those boys at Breton did to me. He said he'd loved me all along, even in high school. But then he changed. It's like all he wanted was to build me up so he could tear me down, bit by bit. I was homeless with a little baby, yet that meant nothing to him. He started telling me I was "damaged goods" and my life was over. If I ever tried to leave, he said me and my bastard child would be pimp bait on the streets. And he was the only person who would ever put up with us. For a long time I believed him, Bright Eyes. I didn't know any different. He hit me all the time and everything. And that makes me even more ashamed than what happened at Breton. But then he made his big mistake. He started hurting my babies.

Bradford got a cast iron pan to the head for that. Oh, he knocked me out cold afterwards, sure as you can say asshole. How I wish I'd been able to kill him! I told Creek to take little Dooley and hide beneath the trailer and then I nailed him as hard as I could. But the fucker was too mean to die. Pardon my French, Bright Eyes. But there are no other words to describe a man like that. The one and only time I found the sheriff by the road, with my head bleeding and the boys at my side, I told him as fast as I could what happened. But all Bradford had to do was roll out his family's pedigree, how he was the son of a rich chemical magnate in Cincinnati and I had a history of mental illness. "Go ahead and check the records at Pinnacle, officer," Bradford bragged. "She's a certified basket case. She makes up stories like this all the time."

Naturally, the sheriff and Brad's father turned out to be friends and belong to the same civic organizations. That's how it is around here, Bright Eyes. I was trapped.

So I taught Creek to be a fighter.

I taught him how to hurt Brad back and protect Dooley. Taught him that his mommy might have been a loser, but not him. The real shining stars in all of this are my two boys.

Why am I writing to you? Because I want you to know, Bright Eyes, how much I love Creek and Dooley. They are my life, more beautiful and shining than I will ever be. And I'll die before I let them lead this life of hell forever. Brad doesn't know it, but I've been collecting his whiskey bottles and throwing them with these notes into the lake. I know it's a long shot, and something tells me you might have helped them get to the right people. Because today, I got one back. It was a typewritten note from a person at Child Protection Services with their logo at the top. They said they're coming. They're going to bring the police and rescue my boys. If something happens to me Bright Eyes, please find this note somehow and take it to my children. Tell them how much I love them. Tell them over and over again, no matter how tired they get of hearing it. Tell them I'll never stop loving them. Not ever, not for a million years.

Caroline's words end in a frightening scrawl that tears off the page, dotted with drops of blood.

"It must have been Dooley," Creek notes, his voice tinged with tremors of barely contained rage. "When our stepdad found her letter, he hauled her outside and started beating her to death. Dooley must have grabbed her paper and taped it against this chair inside the notebook, along with his stuffed bunny. He was used to hiding his favorite toys like that."

Creek appears stunned, his words hardly audible as they leave his mouth. His eyes are glazed, like he's just witnessed everything he ever thought he knew go up in flames.

My guess is that he had no idea Dooley wasn't his real brother—

Or that Caroline loved him *that* much. Enough to sacrifice her life rather than let him be abused anymore.

"Sh-she was trying to save you that day," I stammer. My

own teardrops stain her crumpled letter. "She knew he might try to kill her for—"

"*Did* kill her for…alerting authorities," Creek corrects.

I wince at the finality of that fact.

"Were Child Protection Services really on their way?" I ask him.

Creek nods slowly. He points outside the trailer to the dark canopy of trees above us. When I squint my eyes, I spy several tree stands in the shadows with planks connecting them that he'd probably built as hiding places as a young teen.

"Most people, including law enforcement, don't think to look up," Creek explains. "I nearly killed him, Robin. He totally underestimated my strength—and my rage. When he strangled my mom, I jumped him and began beating him to a pulp. I poured every ounce of hatred I had into breaking his thick head and bones, even though he was twice my size. I was like a whirlwind of anger. But then Dooley came out of the trailer. He saw our mom lying in the grass, dead."

"And you didn't want to kill someone, right in front of… Dooley. Because you didn't want him to become like—"

"*Me*," Creek finishes my sentence. He shakes his head. "Hard. Cold. And too old, too fast."

He draws a deep breath and turns to gaze at the gold reflection that's spreading from the setting sun over Bender Lake.

"Me and Dooley split after that. Right away. I took him up to the tree stands so the police wouldn't find us and break us up. I had a whole network built from limb to limb. All along, though Mom never knew it, I'd been planning for the day to help her escape with us. And it was really strange—I'll never forget how me and Dooley climbed up that tree after her murder. My stepdad managed to flee, and we stayed super quiet. Once the authorities left, this bird, a mourning dove, landed on our tree stand and took off down a trail. It kept cooing, like we were supposed to follow it. And damn if Dooley didn't do exactly that, like it was calling to him. I chased Dooley down the trail that twisted and turned all the way around the lake, until it led to—"

"Granny Tinker?"

Creek turns around to stare at me. His eyes are glistening. "She had the box, Robin. Even way back then, when she didn't know who Caroline was. She'd been collecting things— items I guess the dove must have been taking to her. Like she knew we were coming."

When I hear a coo in the woods, it makes me jump.

I lift Caroline's last letter and hold it out to Creek.

"You never saw this before today. You didn't know how much she really loved you. Can you forgive her...now?"

Inside, I'm shaking with everything I've got. Because if Creek's answer is no, in spite of Caroline jeopardizing her own life to make things better for them, then it's pretty clear to me that he's got an axe to grind against women that I can never truly fix. Granny may have glued together the shards of the Stone of Thieves, but no one can repair Creek if he doesn't want to be whole.

Creek gazes out at the lake again. His features look hard, even in the warm hues that filter through the trees. He's so quiet I wonder if he's breathing.

Yet there's a peculiar red glow seeping into the light around him from inside the broken-down trailer. When I turn to look at its source, I notice the Stone of Thieves on the dining room table is pulsing a brilliant crimson. As I step to peer closer, I can tell one of the star-like cracks in the center has fused together, ever so slightly.

And the sight brings tears to my eyes.

❧ 11 ❧

Creek doesn't say anything—just lets this moment of glimpsing into his mother's soul linger—as we walk hand in hand toward the golden light that spreads across Bender Lake. The setting sun colors his features a little, but what really strikes me is the slight softness at the corners of his normally ice-blue eyes. Maybe this is what forgiveness looks like, I wonder. Not completely, but enough to at least to be willing to understand why Caroline did what she did. Creek holds the Stone of Thieves in his hand, radiating so much now it pulses red through his fingers, and I'm pretty certain I know what he's ready to do. Sure enough, when we reach the shore, Creek tugs at my hand and we sit down on the sand, the air around us punctuated by the sound of lapping waves. He sets the gleaming ruby heart between us, and we both glance at the lake for a moment that mirrors the trees and our faces. Creek simply nods.

He's prepared now, I can tell, to see what happened to

Caroline and Sherwood after the twister. To discover more about who she really was. We both take deep breaths and hold the warm stone together. Before the two of us can blink, we're already there...

We see Caroline in her room at Pinnacle. Her hair's disheveled and she's in white flannel pajamas, unfolding a piece of paper in her hands. Scanning it for a moment, her lips turn up in a smile and she begins to read aloud:

Dear Miss Caroline,

You say you don't want me to be gallant, but I can't help it. Yes, we were knocked out in that storm. When I woke up and saw you stirring, I carried you to the VW and bulleted back for Cincinnati, wondering if I should take you to a hospital. But you started talking to me non-stop, remember? It was like some dam burst in your heart. You giggled like a little girl and thrust your arm out the window, waving your hand up and down and saying now you know what it's like to fly. God, it was nice to see you smile.

No wonder the wind carried you so far. You're a featherweight. I know, because I hoisted you over my shoulders and took you up the ladder back into your room at Pinnacle. Ten o'clock sharp! See, I keep my promises. You giggled at that, too. You pointed at the clock and said you were going to memorize this moment because it was the best night of your life. For once, you felt free. I hope we can have more nights like this, Caroline. Where we step outside everything our schools tell us to be. After all, Dr. Cutler says we're crazy. So we might as well enjoy it, right?

When you wake up tomorrow morning, hopefully you'll find this letter under your pillow. I want to show you the art we created. It's magnificent. I found it about fifty yards from where we fell. I store my works in the groundskeeper's building between Pinnacle and Breton. Mr. Flanagan, the gardener, doesn't tell. You can meet me there after your appointment with Dr. Cutler on Wednesday. The schools expect us to study in the library after that, so no one will miss us.

Thanks for being my muse, Caroline. I'm bowing right now because I know you hate it. Someday you'll remember that and think it's funny.

— SHERWOOD

P.S. Better burn this letter so the PP won't find it. God knows, they live for that shit.

Caroline laughs when she reaches the end of the letter, but she doesn't rip it into shreds or light a match for it to burn. Instead, she walks over to her window and opens it. She coos softly into the air, and soon, a dove lands on the sill, where she feeds it some peanuts that she'd saved, lying on her dresser. Then she talks quietly to the bird and strokes the back of its head. Rolling Sherwood's letter into a thin cylinder, she holds it out, watching the dove take it into its small beak. The bird lifts its wings and alights into the air. "Bye Bright Eyes," Caroline calls out, watching the dove disappear into the morning sky.

The next thing we see, Caroline is in her uniform in Dr. Cutler's office. She's sitting on a chair with her hands folded and her back rod straight, staring at the floor while he talks nearly non-stop.

"You understand, of course, that you're prone to delusions. Things that never really happened. You can't always trust what you think you see—right, Caroline? Just like your grandmother. How's that medication been working out?"

"Um, I'm not sure," Caroline says with a slight smirk, avoiding his gaze. "The other day, when there was a tornado warning, I saw a funnel coming in the distance. It had a red, almost glowing eye in the center. And it turned, like it was looking straight at me."

She lifts her chin and stares Dr. Cutler dead in the eye.

"And suddenly, I felt more alive than ever before. It was exhilarating—all that color, energy, and force swirling at me like…destiny. I was petrified. But there was something magical about it, too. As if it were from a dream. It didn't seem of this world."

Caroline's eyes narrow, her lips rising little, as if challenging him.

"Do you think that's a delusion too, Dr. Cutler? Or do you think that nature might call to us like that sometimes, if we're open to it. I mean, if we can step beyond our usual routines…"

Dr. Cutler shuffles his feet in his chair, appearing nervous for a moment from Caroline's peculiar burst of confidence, as though the power balance between them has shifted. He clears his throat, then slips on his reading glasses like a shield. The light from the window reflects off the frames so you can no longer see his eyes. For a long time, he scribbles onto his notepad.

"I-I think it's a sign I need to up your medication," Dr. Cutler finally replies in an authoritative tone. Without returning her gaze, he reaches into his desk drawer to fetch a vial of more pills. "It's clear to me that you need more rest,

Caroline," he nods, handing her the bottle. "And if you ever spot another—what did you call it? Red eye in a storm? Well, I want you to make another appointment with me. Immediately—"

"Sure thing, Doc," Caroline replies with an innocent, lilting voice, rising to leave.

As she exits his office and closes the door, she looks both ways down the empty hall to double check if anyone's there. Smiling as if she holds a secret, she strides happily toward a door at the other end and along the way dumps her pills in the trash. The minute she leaves the building, she begins to run, laughing with her arms outstretched, toward the groundskeeper's building.

The old garden warehouse is made of stone, as gothic as the rest of Caroline's boarding school, and flanked on all sides by tall shade trees. Caroline scans the front mahogany door before trying the brass knob, only to discover it's locked. She inhales a long breath, hoping no one has spotted her, and ducks behind a large hardwood tree, waiting. Something begins to tickle at her hair, and she pulls at a strand, discovering a leaf. When she yanks it out, another leaf drops and tumbles into her eyes, then another. Soon, she's barraged with falling green leaves. Shaking her head, she glances up and spots Sherwood high on a limb, laughing.

"You know what's great about hiding in trees?" Sherwood calls down with a lop-sided grin. "Most people don't think to look up."

He leaps to her side, startling her.

"Give me your foot," Sherwood says, cradling his hands together to make a stirrup.

"What?" asks Caroline.

"Your foot, m'lady." He offers her a florid bow, in spite of her rolled eyes, and kneels, pointing to a window. "I'm going to give you a boost." Sherwood positions his hands as a stirrup again.

"Oh!" Caroline giggles, glancing up. "Guess you don't have a key to the door, huh?" She eyes the slightly open window, obscured from the street level by thick trees, with hesitation. "You really think I'll fit?"

"Sure! I've done it a hundred times. One—two—three—up!"

With that, Sherwood vaults Caroline high enough to cling to the bottom of the windowsill, watching her wriggle through.

"I didn't know you wear purple underwear!" He laughs, glimpsing for a second up her uniform skirt. "Kind of cute—"

All at once, he hears a thud. "Guess that means you landed?"

Sherwood takes a few steps back and makes a running leap for the window, swiftly hoisting himself inside like he's done this many times before. He lands on his feet beside Caroline, who's laying flat on the cold, stone floor. Her eyes are shut and she's immobile.

"Oh my god—you okay?" Sherwood leans over, cradling her face. "C-Caroline?" He gets no response. He pats her cheek gently and searches her eyes. "Caroline! Baby! Can you hear me?"

Caroline bursts into laughter, the sound echoing inside the warehouse.

"*Baby?*" She ribs him. "You must have been really worried—"

"I didn't know you had that in you!" Sherwood bursts, aghast. But then he collapses into laughing with her. "You're a total sneak." A slight blush suffuses his cheeks.

"No I'm not," Caroline breathes, her lips a mere inch from his face. "This is just the real me. Before Pinnacle started doing a number on my head. I used to have a sense of humor, you know."

Her eyes twinkle as she stares into his that are wide with surprise. "After third grade, we moved and I grew up in the hillbilly ghetto over in Lower Price Hill. Where all the folks from the hollers go to live in Cincinnati. My parents were gone and my grandma worked all the time. So I sorta ran around the neighborhood wild. Catching fireflies, playing kick the can, staying out so late I'd finally come home and land on the bed I shared with my grandma in a heap. When I arrived here, Pinnacle tried to convince me there was something wrong with that girl. She has dirty knees and she's unruly and she's got to have her wings clipped. They gave me speech lessons till I wanted to cry. Hours of etiquette training, everything." Caroline surprises Sherwood with a soft kiss on the cheek. "But you brought her back," she whispers.

Before Sherwood can react, Caroline is up like a sprite, dashing past the gardeners's truck and mowers to the other end of the warehouse where rows of canvases are lined up against a wall.

"C'mon!" she cries. "I wanna see your art. I wanna see everything wonderful and wild that I've been missing since I came here. Show me what you got!"

Half-dazed, Sherwood shakes his head for a second, getting accustomed to this new, wild girl who'd been unleashed. His lips stretch into a smirk while his fingers linger over the spot on his cheek where Caroline kissed him. He untangles his long legs, rising slowly, and jogs over to the paintings.

Displayed against sacks of grass seed and fertilizer, sandwiched between hand-held mowers and rakes, are over a dozen homemade canvases stretched upon wood frames. Each painting is a fury of chaotic color and composition. One has angry black lines, thick as prison bars, over the window of a dark, gothic building that appears to trap lost souls. Another is a splatter of disjointed paint drippings with broad swaths of crimson that connect them together like blood. Still others are abstract, random circles that swirl and overlap each other in clashing streams of confusion. The only thing that they appear to have in common is that they're…crazy.

"Work of a madman, huh?" Sherwood remarks, glancing at Caroline. "Mr. Flanagan says my art only makes sense to him when he's high. He does a lot of weed around here, and sometimes harder stuff, when he can get it. We sort of have a deal. I don't rat to the administration about his little… addictions," Sherwood nods at the paintings, "and he doesn't mention a peep about mine."

Caroline admires the paintings with a mixture of awe and fascination on her face.

"So, um," Sherwood utters a bit nervously, glancing aside. "W-What do you think?"

Caroline narrows her eyes and peers slowly across the entire row of paintings, registering each one.

"They're…they're beautiful," she finally gasps.

She steps closer, tilting some of the canvases forward so she can see more of his work. But then her gaze alights on one canvas, squeezed between two other larger paintings, and it makes her breath halt. It's a soft depiction of a nude, young blonde woman, created in great detail with tender strokes of blue flowing paint, the same color as the petals of the forget-me-nots that are scattered around the lovely figure like rain. The young woman appears sad and glances up at the petals as though she wishes she could join them in the sky. Her body is slim, yet her breasts and hips are slightly swollen with blossoming maturity—a young woman on the cusp of adulthood. The shock on Caroline's face betrays her realization that Sherwood must have painted this a while ago —before they'd even met.

She whips around angrily and pins him with her stare.

"Sh-Sherwood," her voice quakes a little. "Did you lie to me? Have you been watching me in my room all along? *Stalking* me?"

Sherwood shuffles his feet and focuses on the floor. When his eyes rise to meet hers, they're filled with so much longing it makes her tremble.

He scans the painting and becomes absorbed by the outline of the beautiful young woman, every curve of her cheek, breasts and hips, as though he's stepping inside the colors.

"There's...there's a price to being the most beautiful girl in Cincinnati," he confesses softly, almost in a whisper. "Boys dream of you. Spin stories about you. And paint you without your knowledge."

He lifts his eyes to meet hers, not as a stranger, but as someone who knows every inch of her softest places too well.

"I did see you naked, Caroline," Sherwood admits. "But it was in my imagination."

Caroline is so still she doesn't appear to be breathing.

Her gaze is indecipherable—as though perhaps not even she knows who she is right now. That wandering child from a hillbilly neighborhood who ran free and wild, or the prim young woman who accepts everything her school tells her so her stale future will be secured. Caroline purses her lips for a moment and runs her fingers down the narrow pleats of her uniform skirt, examining the fabric closely and removing a piece of lint. Then she draws a deep breath, and to Sherwood's surprise, she stares him straight in the eye and raises her chin. Her fingers work the buttons of her uniform blouse and unwrap it over her shoulders before unclasping her bra from behind.

Perfect, small breasts spill from her white starched blouse. Caroline glances at her cleavage. "You missed a mole here," she says, brushing a fingertip over the dip between her breasts. "If you're going to be an artist, you'd sure as hell better get it right."

Now it's Sherwood who appears breathless.

For a long time, he simply stares at her raw beauty, as though stunned. But Caroline doesn't say a word. Her entire being is challenge, and beauty, and something fierce and wild that Sherwood looks like he's never seen before and couldn't possibly name. Impulsively, he grabs a paint brush by his feet and raises it to his lips, taking a lick to wet the bristles. With slow steps, as though approaching something untamed, he moves closer and gazes into her eyes with an expression that appears to be asking permission. Without glancing down,

Caroline unbuttons and slips her skirt over her hips, and it lands with her underwear to the floor. She steps out of her uniform like it's an outworn skin.

Sherwood's hand seems to tremble as he traces the paintbrush lightly between her breasts, over the mole she spoke of. Caroline closes her eyes, relishing the contact with her skin. Goose bumps surface on her chest.

"Paint me," she breathes into his ear. "Paint the *real* me that only you can see. Bring me back, Sherwood."

Sherwood's eyes are wide, and in that moment, he appears every inch the 17-year-old boy Caroline knows him to be. When he dares to trace her nipple with his paintbrush, she stops his hand cold.

"No," she whispers, tossing the paintbrush aside. It clatters to the floor.

Sherwood's eyes appear downcast for a moment. He nods at her refusal, dropping his hand. He doesn't glance up, as though her physical beauty is so extraordinary it actually hurts.

Caroline smiles. "With your tongue, silly," she whispers.

The look in Sherwood's eyes is pure awe. Slowly, he takes her nipple in his mouth and Caroline leans her head back and smiles. He works his way to her other breast. She softly groans, lifting her ribcage as though craving more. Swiftly, she unbuttons his Breton oxford shirt and slips her hands beneath the fabric, relishing the feel of his chest. She clutches him to her—hard. Sherwood dives for her lips as she tears off his shirt. Her hands work every part of him, his shoulders, abs, and then his back, before pulling him down to their soft bed of discarded clothes.

"Paint me with your body," Caroline demands. Her hands rise to cup his face and she kisses him.

Sherwood removes his jeans and underwear and slides his hands over the luxurious swell of her hips, admiring every inch of her skin. He lifts his hand to stroke her wheat-blond hair, spiraling a soft strand through his fingers. Then he traces her small breasts with a lock of her hair, like one of his paintbrushes, before he kisses them again. He steals a long kiss from her lips, pulling her face to his before reaching his hand very gently to her sex. To his surprise, she fondles him back. She's so wet, his fingers slide up and down easily along the folds between her thighs, and he circles her nipples with his other hand until Caroline leans her head back and is moaning again.

"Caroline...Caroline," he whispers, so erect now he can barely stand it. His hand brushes her hair from her face and he cups her cheek, gazing into her eyes. "Be mine. Now. Okay?"

"Maybe," she smiles, tenderly running her fingers over his hardness till his eyes close and he nearly comes. "But only if you're a *true* artist."

Sherwood offers her a knowing nod. He leans down to her sex to please her with his tongue. With each stroke she begins to moan louder and louder. He's undulating, watching her back arc as she feels pleasure in waves. At that moment, he runs his hands over her thighs, her hips, her small waist—as though painting each part of her with the color of his need.

"Now?" he begs. "Do you have pro—"

"I'm on the pill," she cuts in. "Dr. Cutler insists, since I'm supposed to be white trash. You know how girls like that are—"

"One man's trash is another's…," Sherwood drifts off, carefully weighing his words. "What I mean is, a girl like you was born to be treasured, Caroline," he says without a hint of sarcasm. His searing blue eyes appear to fall into hers. "You're everything I ever wanted. You can't blame me for painting you in my heart—"

All at once, her lips crush against his, swallowing him, as though she's the one who controls their desire. Sherwood enters her and begins thrusting—harder and harder—in a storm of strength. Her body replies to his with shockwaves of arching rhythm. As Caroline sways, she runs her hands through his long brown hair, working her fingers toward his back and kneading at his muscles. Then she clutches him for dear life and moans, over and over. As Sherwood's motion comes to a stop, he gasps for breath and collapses onto her soft breasts.

Caroline strokes his hair with a smile on her face, as if he belongs to her now. Her fingers brush against his cheek. "You're not a bad artist," she whispers tenderly.

Sherwood doesn't answer. He merely nuzzles against her chest. When he lifts his eyes to hers, they twinkle with combination of awe and mischief. "You are, too. But then, you've had a little practice, huh?"

"*Every* girl from my old neighborhood has had practice," Caroline smirks. "So have you."

He traces a lock of her hair to her chin and swipes a kiss. "Whatever makes great art is worth it, right? As long as you end up with a masterpiece." Sherwood stubbornly ignores her rolled eyes at his grandiose remark. "Speaking of which," he says excitedly, "do you wanna see our painting?"

He stands to his feet, naked, and grabs a canvas nearby that glistens a little, the paint appearing still slightly wet.

"What do you think?" he asks. He shuffles his bare feet on the floor, appearing a bit nervous.

Caroline sits up and hugs her knees to her chest, hiding her breasts. "Well, I like the *frame*."

Sherwood recalls, in that very moment, that he's still nude. He blushes a little, but holds his ground.

"Well, maybe this artwork should be in the raw. But do you like it, M-Miss Caroline?"

She admires his muscles and lithe body, the long, messy strands of honey-brown hair that fall into his eyes. "Sure, I like what I see," she teases. Then she takes in the wild splatters of paint from the cans he'd set up that day, along with shreds of corn husks and wood chips cast by the tornado's fury. There are barn nails wedged into the canvas from the violent force of wind, rusty screws and hinges. Yet most curious of all is the way the paint swirls into tight circles at the upper left edge, as though it were spun like a top.

"It-it looks like...," Caroline pauses for a moment, stumbling for words, "like power in motion. Maybe even the fingerprint of...God," she says carefully.

She examines the red eye depicted in the center of the painting, a still marble in the midst of chaos, wide and round as though it's staring at her. A shiver works its way through her body. "You know," she says quietly, "we could have gotten killed—"

"We nearly *were*," Sherwood responds gravely.

He sets the painting down against a seed bag and returns to Caroline, sitting beside her and wrapping his arms around her thin frame and hugging her close. Together, they study the red orb at the center of the painting.

"That's never happened to me before," Sherwood confesses. "I've never gotten that close to a twister. And I've only heard about the red eye in stories from my grandfather. I thought they were legends. When you pointed it out to me that evening, the red glow inside all that spinning chaos, I felt like it was staring at us. Maybe even daring us, somehow. But for what, I don't know."

"I do," Caroline whispers.

She remains silent for a while, still gazing at the red center of the painting as though listening to it.

"I-I heard it that day," she admits. "Out of the roar, I heard a word in a deep voice. Almost like a heavy humming."

"What did it say?" Sherwood asks, stunned. He turns to her, his expression wide open with fascination.

Caroline remains still, her gaze enigmatic. She brushes a long lock of hair from his face before giving him a kiss.

"Live," she replies.

She searches his eyes.

"Sherwood," she asks. "Do you think we're crazy?"

Sherwood nods. "Yeah," he says, "I do." He returns her kiss. "But sometimes crazy's the only way out. Next Wednesday night, meet me here. Okay? I really want to introduce you to somebody. I think you'll like him. And he can explain everything."

The ruby heart's so hot between our hands we have to drop it.

"I hate him!" Creek bursts, standing up. "That asshole Sherwood knocked her up! I bet those weren't birth control pills at all—they were something else the doctor gave her to keep her medicated. And then Sherwood probably *left* her!"

He crisscrosses the shore with furious strides, kicking up sand.

"All that talk about love and art was total bullshit. To get under her skin. Sure, Bradford Helms beat the crap out of her, but Sherwood broke her first! You can tell—she really loved him, dammit! Some rich boy with nothing to lose, just like Bradford—"

He picks up the ruby heart from its place on the sand and throws it hard into the middle of the lake. A column of steam instantly rises where the stone hits the water.

I kick off my shoes and dash into the lake, running with all my might. Yet my legs feel heavy and slow, like I'm attempting to run despite the gravity on a planet like Jupiter.

The ruby heart holds the key—I know it! I stretch out my arms and spin them in swift, swimming strokes, kicking as hard as I can to try and reach the stone before it falls to the bottom of the lake. All at once, I feel Creeks muscular arm lock around my neck and waist, pulling me to his chest. I should've known he'd catch up with me in a heartbeat. Startled, I hit him, but it's no use—he's got me like a vise.

"Stop—stop it! Let me go!" I cry, slamming my elbow into his ribs. Creek throws me off easily and grabs my shoulders, dog paddling to keep us afloat. It's no trouble for him, with his long, strong legs, but I'm not about to have it. I wail at his chest with my fists anyway.

"Dammit—if we don't retrieve that stone somehow and find out what really happened to Caroline, I'm outta here! I can't take this anymore, Creek! I'm leaving all your hurt and pain and anger behind that fills our lives like toxic smoke."

I turn to watch the steam still rising from the lake. The vapor glows in an eerie red column that reaches to the sky. In that moment, I hear wild screeches—the sound of a bird gone haywire. The noise is deafening, like the hysterical cheeping from that creepy Alfred Hitchcock bird movie. Then a splash erupts in the water. A dove rises from the lake, flapping its wings madly with a chain in its beak, the ruby heart glistening in the sun. The dove makes an abrupt turn, as though obeying some kind of invisible radar. It flies northwest with the Stone of Thieves dangling back and forth like a pendulum in the air.

Shivers work their way over my whole body. Before I know

it, Creek has me cradled in his arms. He hugs me tight and is carrying me as he walks to the shore. For a second, he swivels to watch the dove grow smaller and smaller on the horizon. Then he bows his forehead against mine.

"Robin," he whispers tenderly, "I don't care about any damn bird or stone. All I care about is *you*."

His passion and intensity are almost more than I can take. I shut my eyes, shielding myself from this soul I love so much—more than anything. Yet his anger can be beyond scary and pushes me to the breaking point sometimes. I feel Creek stroke the strands of my wet hair away from my face. "Baby," he whispers. "Oh, baby…"

When I open my eyes, I'm lying on the warm sand, the sun striking my cheek. Creek slinks on top of me and gives me a gentle kiss, our wet bodies sealed against each other like one being. He lifts a scraggly wet strand of hair from my cheek.

"I love you so much, Robin," he whispers, kissing me again. "Whatever you want. Whatever you ask. I'll do." He twirls the gold wedding ring around my finger. "You're my wife. If you really want to go after that stupid stone, we'll go."

He scoops the back of my head from the sand and draws me into a kiss. A kiss that says he's sorry. A kiss that says he needs me forever. And maybe that's all I can really ask for.

"But shouldn't we see where the bird's flying to?" I press anyway, hearing the plea in my own voice.

Creek sighs and turns to gaze out over the lake. His eyes trace the path of the wings that are evaporating in the distance. "I know *exactly* where that dove's going," he nods.

"Where's that?" I ask, puzzled.

"Where it always goes," he replies. "Back to Caroline."

🎄 13 🎄

Creek kick starts his motorcycle, filling the air with an ear-splitting roar, and I hop on. The machine snorts and bucks like a wild beast. Yet as soon as he slips on a pair of leather gloves and we steer onto the hidden, brambled paths around Bender Lake, and then onto the wider backroads at higher speeds, the Indian purrs contentedly. We head northwest toward Cincinnati, into the darkness.

The sun's almost gone now as we hit the main highway, and I know by the time we reach the city it will be night. It's always hard for me to return to the area where I grew up. To the lonely person I was when I left there, the day my dad had a stroke and I stole a car to bust him out of the hospital to keep him from being arrested. That girl I left behind was a spoiled brat, yet starving for true affection. She had all the diamonds you could want and not a flicker of light left in her soul. Now, my relationships are *real*. They may still be rocky—but hell, at least I'm real, too. I grip Creek's waist tighter and feel his warm hand squeeze against mine for a moment. Never in my wildest dreams did I think I could have the love of a guy like Creek. The whole reason we're making this trip is because of love. He's willing to face hell—the truth about his past and his own mom—just to keep me.

But the person I know as *me* has changed.

No longer do I want to shop at Fountain Square downtown, or check out the newest jewelry collection at Tiffany's, because I have everything I need. Right here, warm and muscular, beneath my hands on this godforsaken, rebuilt motorcycle. But that doesn't mean my stomach doesn't clench after an hour when I spy the pulsing artery of lights from cars dashing in and out of the heart of the city. This town can break people. It did my father. And my old neighborhood of Indian Hill, despite its titanic mansions and marbled columns, is filled with more levels of emotional wasteland than Mother Superior at Pinnacle promised waits for us beyond the gates of Hades. I suck in a deep breath, watching the sights speed past me in a flurry of memories as we travel beneath the sparkling street lamps of the city's poshest avenues. Nearing the silhouettes of the tall spires of Pinnacle and Breton in the early moonlight, I'm struck by their imposing structures—so high they interrupt the stars. Only a few lights twinkle in their dorms, because most kids are still in the dining hall right now or studying in the libraries. For some reason, I expect Creek to stop and hide his motorcycle in the thick hedges near Pinnacle. But he keeps on going, heading towards Breton.

He brings the motorcycle to a halt beside some bushes near one of Breton's administrative buildings. I don't know what hunch Creek's following this time, till I see a pair of wings gliding past a street lamp—and the glow of the red heart dangling from a beak. How did Creek know? I wonder. We hop off the Indian, and Creek rams it inside a dense bush that swallows it in leaves.

"There's your friend," Creek says, pointing up. I squint at the dark building, barely making out a bird perched on the windowsill. The Stone of Thieves appears to be lying at its feet, radiating on the ledge like a taillight.

Yet I'm not sure Bright Eyes is my friend at all.

What does this bird want? What will we find at Breton?

I sigh, tapping Creek on the shoulder.

"Why are we here?" I ask him. "It's not like anyone's going to tell us what happened."

Creek nods, raking his hand through his windblown hair. He glances up at the Breton office building.

"Because," he reasons, "there'll be records that say what became of rich-boy Sherwood, buried somewhere around this place. It's like the textbooks back in school—they always record the comings and goings of the wealthy. But a poor, scholarship girl like Caroline," he sighs, "well, I wouldn't be surprised if her name got scrubbed from their records the minute she left, like she never attended here. They probably viewed her as an embarrassment. Sherwood's records are the only lead we have."

Creek studies the tall building, flanked by gargoyles with fangs bared that appear to be snarling in the moonlight.

I forgot how much those stone creatures scare me. My pulse picks up at the sight.

But what scares me more is seeing Creek stride toward an

unlit corner of the dark building. He takes a flying leap toward the stone edge to begin scaling the wall.

With his powerful hands and carefully placed feet.

I hear the echo of a mournful cry as the dove flies off into the night. It leaves the ruby heart behind.

"I'll let you know what I find out," Creek calls down to me. He's several feet above ground already and hanging onto the ledges and cracks between the stones by his fingertips and toes. His sheer, raw strength shouldn't come as a surprise to me any more—especially when he's as determined as hell. But I can't control the shivers that skitter down my spine.

Screw it! I say to myself. If Creek can do this without falling, then so can I—

I hope…

"Hold on! I'm coming up," I call back to him. My knees are trembling, and for all I know we might both fall to our deaths. But as Creek always says, at least we'll be together.

"That's my girl," Creek's voice finds me in the darkness, giving me assurance.

I set my hands on the cold stones of the Breton building, forcing myself to climb up that first step and maintain my courage, no matter what.

Then I claw my fingers around the next higher stones, and the next, cramming the toes of my sneakers into the cracks.

And I can practically hear Creek smiling in the night.

Creek yanks me through the window into an unlit office room

at Breton, where I stumble to my feet. He has the ruby heart in his leather-gloved hands, dangling by its silver chain. The door to the room is closed, and we're in shadows, as quiet as church mice. All around us are filing cabinets and wide binders on rows of shelves, but we have no flashlight, nothing. Creek says he never brings lights or weapons when breaking and entering an official place of business, so there's less chance of doing federal time—if caught. Where he ditched his gun he didn't tell me. And there's no way to know if this office actually holds the records we're looking for.

What's more, the stone has gone cold now, unwilling to betray its secrets.

Part of me wonders if this is a total goose chase. But as Creek scans the room and walks toward the door, the ruby heart begins to pulse again. Its soft glow is no brighter than a candle. Creek turns to look at me, nodding at the stone like it's his compass. The closer he steps to the door, the more vivid its color appears.

"This way," he whispers, unlocking the door.

We skulk through the hall. At any moment I'm ready to bolt back down the side of the building if someone stumbles upon us. Quietly, we follow the flickers of the stone, step by step, trying to gauge the strength of its glow. Edging to the left makes it become dimmer—cloudy. While edging to the right makes the radiance intensify till it's as bright as an emergency dome light. It's eerie to watch the stone's red corona lead us forward, like some kind of devil's lantern. When we enter another dark hallway, and step near the third door to the right, the stone becomes so hot Creek has to let it fall to the floor.

"Must be here," he whispers.

Creek tries the knob, but the door we've reached is locked.

For reasons I don't quite understand, Creek threads the necklace between his teeth. He bites down as hard on the chain as he can and twists it over his molars. Then he holds the necklace between his fingers and straightens out a link so it's as flat as a wire. He does it again and again until he has several links that he fastens to each other like a long poker. Bending down, he inserts his handmade tool into the knob to pick the lock like a seasoned professional. I hear a subtle click, and Creek smiles, turning the knob and swinging the door open wide.

Immediately, I get the chills.

All around us are filing cabinets and binders on shelves, like the other room. But the difference now is that the Stone of Thieves is so bright, it's as though we're peering through an infra-red scope. Creek holds the ruby heart by his shirtsleeve to keep it from burning through his glove, and he quickly closes the blinds on the window so no one will see us. When he takes a step back near a file cabinet, the ruby heart begins to smoke through his flannel cuff. He turns over a metal trash can and sets the stone on top, blowing out his sleeve. Turning to me, his eyes search mine.

"Do you want to pull open the file cabinet Robin, or should I?"

I pause, taking in the gravity of his request.

Inside that ordinary, gray cabinet is quite possibly the truth.

The facts about Sherwood's life—

Whether he graduated from Breton. Or went on to become an innovative artist, the way he dreamed.

Maybe whether he got Caroline pregnant, if the records dare to mention a low-class girl like her, and then ditched her the way Creek believes.

There might be information on his family, where they live, or if anything Sherwood said about their wealth and status were actually true. Or if all his acts of gallantry were really some kind of sham, and he was just as poor as Creek's mother all along.

Can Creek handle the truth of Sherwood Flynn? The man who may well be his father?

I stare at the metal file cabinet like it's Pandora's Box, full of secrets that could surprise us or change our lives.

Or is it more like that black box they find in the wreckage after an airplane crash, which reveals the sad truth about people's demise?

I chew my lip and stand a little taller, then nod at Creek, preparing to open this mystery for him.

"I got this," I say with as much boldness as I can muster. I hold out my hand for his glove.

But when I cover my palm and give the handle a yank, it refuses to yield to my fingers.

I pull harder, several times, but it won't budge. It's locked—

"Step back," Creek warns.

Before I can ask him what for, he slams his fist into the side of the filing cabinet with such force that the metal buckles at the front, wedging open a corner of the cabinet.

And the ruby heart shines so bright, I fear the trash can might melt like wax to the floor.

"This is it, baby," Creek nods, rubbing his knuckles without flinching.

He takes the glove back from me and slips his hand inside, then reaches into the open edge to pull out a file.

Finch, Rutger, the label says at the top. *Graduated.*

Fleck, Hurston, the next file he pulls out reads. *Transferred.*

Flynn, Sherwood, the file after that one states. *Deactivated—*

Creek lifts that file from the cabinet with ginger fingers as though it's priceless and opens it up so I can see by the light of the crimson glow of the stone.

"Sherwood Alastair Flynn the Fifth," Creek reads aloud, scanning Sherwood's entry and exit dates from Breton, which drop off at almost the end of his senior year. "Diagnosis: Bi-Polar Disorder with Hallucinatory Tendencies. Examined by Dr. Harold Cutler, Psychiatrist."

So they *did* claim Sherwood was as crazy as a loon.

Creek threads his gloved finger over the next paragraph, which details Sherwood's IQ of 140+ and his over-the-top scores on the ACT and SAT exams, despite a poor attendance record. Every ivy-league college on the east coast had already sent him scholarship offers. The paragraph after that mentions his family has resided in Indian Hill for six generations and founded the Cincinnati Federal Bank in the mid-nineteenth century.

Holy shit!

My mouth drops at the sight of those words.

Cincinnati Federal was the same bank we robbed! Where Laura Ritter's dad is the bank president, who once gave me a tour while I was at Pinnacle. Who knew that the Flynn family —and Creek's possible kin—are the actual *owners?* Lucky for them, Creek eventually returned the money so we wouldn't get caught…

I check Creek's gaze, but he seems totally unimpressed by this coincidence—and by the fact that he might not have come from a long line of poor white trash after all. Instead, he's completely focused on something more compelling he sees on the rest of the page. Creek's finger traces to the bottom of the typewritten form where large red letters are stamped over the last paragraph of the document with the following word:

DECEASED.

And I feel as though I've taken a bullet to my gut.

I begin shaking, trying to hide it from Creek—

I don't know why this comes as such a shock. Sherwood was certainly an adrenaline junky, and he loved taking risks. Next to the red stamp is a date in May, right before the end of the Breton school year.

So Sherwood *died* before he could graduate?

Tears well up that I blink back with all my might. I glance at Creek and search his blue eyes that are as confused as mine.

Creek's jaw muscles twist in strain, but he's refusing to show any emotion right now. He pulls out a photocopy from beneath the form of one of Sherwood's paintings. It's the depiction he created of the red eye at the center of the twister, which he showed to Caroline the first time they made love. We gaze at it through the crimson light of the stone, which pulses now to the rhythm of a heartbeat, and it makes the red eye in the middle almost look like it's blinking at us. Goosebumps alight on my skin as Creek's eyes raise to meet mine. He leans down to grab the ruby heart by his shirtsleeve and holds the bright stone out to me.

And I know, beyond a shadow of a doubt, if I touch that stone, we'll both see what happened to Sherwood and Caroline.

Heart racing, I tuck my hand inside my sleeve.

Then I lay it over the hot and throbbing Stone of Thieves.

14

I t's late at night.

Sherwood is walking stealthily, ducking from shadow to shadow like a phantom near the gardener's building between Pinnacle and Breton, avoiding the glare of the occasional street lamp. He has a canvas tucked beneath his arm, which he clings to protectively. Looking both ways, he dashes across a patch of moonlit lawn to the side of the gardener's building that's concealed by heavy trees. He carefully sets down the painting and runs his fingers along the cracks between the stones of the building, up and down, then over and across, until he pauses with a smile. Pulling out a crumpled note, he opens it to read by the light of the moon.

In words written by hand with a purple pen, the note says, *Look up, silly.*

All at once, Caroline lands from her tree-limb perch on her feet beside Sherwood, startling him.

"You're not the only master of disguise," she giggles.

Sherwood surprises Caroline by grabbing her shoulders and pulling her in for a kiss—long and intense, as though he'd been dying to see her again.

"Maybe not," he breaks off and gazes into her eyes. Cupping her face, he kisses her again with such impetuousness that she rocks back on her heels. "But I'll bet my mischief's more memorable—"

"Try me," Caroline pulls away, tilting her chin and challenging him.

Sherwood's lop-sided grin creases his cheek.

"I want to whisk you away tonight. To meet my grandfather. He's means the world to me. You game?"

"Is that why you brought your painting?" Caroline points to the canvas against the building.

Sherwood nods. "Grandpa was a storm chaser long before me," he replies. "And he was the first one in our family to see the red eye."

"What's his name?" Caroline asks. "Does he live around here?"

"Same name as me," Sherwood smirks. He gives Caroline a ridiculous bow before she socks him in the shoulder, making him laugh. "Sherwood Alastair Flynn the Fourth. I'm the Fifth. And yeah," he sighs. "I guess you could say he lives around here. Within walking distance, in fact. Ready?"

Caroline shrugs with a nod, and Sherwood picks up his painting and takes her by the hand. They tiptoe carefully in stretches of shadows, beside buildings or beneath the canopies of tall trees, until they pass the grounds of the schools.

Crouching down so no one in the local street traffic can spot them, they wait till all is clear and then bolt across the avenue in front of Pinnacle and Breton to an old building. It looks it was built in the same era as their boarding schools, and could even be an annex. Just before they walk around to the front of the stone building, Sherwood stops and leans down to pick a small bouquet of wildflowers.

He holds them up to Caroline in the moonlight, a handful of forget-me-nots.

"It's tradition to bring flowers when you visit someone in a hospital," he explains.

"Hospital?" Caroline says, confused. "There aren't any medical facilities near here. Most of them are over by Mount Auburn. You know, Pill Hill—"

"Not if you're rich, sweetheart," Sherwood points out. "And you don't want anyone to know about your crazy relations who're locked up in the psyche ward. Forget-me-nots are my grandpa's favorite flower, by the way. He always makes me promise never to forget him or what he saw. And believe me, I couldn't. Come on, when you meet him, you'll find out why."

Sherwood gives her a tug on the hand, and they walk around the building to the front door, where a portly, middle-aged doorman in full black and white uniform, complete with a coat that has tails, stands guard over the building. To Caroline's surprise, the doorman simply nods at Sherwood and says "Good evening, Mr. Flynn. Nice flowers again."

"Thanks Mr. Barry," Sherwood smiles as the doorman turns to press several digits into a keypad that makes the front door unlock. He opens it wide for the two of them and bows, motioning for Sherwood and Caroline to enter. Sherwood returns the man's gesture with his own exaggerated bow that features flowing arm movements. Unsure quite what to do, Caroline gives a quick curtsy before Sherwood yanks on her hand to dart inside.

"Is that why you started doing those silly bows?" Caroline whispers as they walk across the marble floor of the lobby, flanked by tall, sculpted columns and gold-framed paintings of distinguished-looking men and women on the walls. Their faces appear mildly bored and disapproving.

Sherwood turns to her and smirks.

"Yep," he replies. "I've been sneaking out of school to come here for visits since I was ten. Nobody ever told me I wasn't supposed to bow back. I thought it was a game that you played to see who could bow the best, and Mr. Barry always indulged me. He's a very dear man, Caroline. More kind to me than my father ever was. And he never betrays our secrets."

"Secrets?" Caroline echoes, still taking in the grandeur of the building.

"Yeah, like the fact that my family is full of nutcases. The kind of people who jump off cliffs to see if they can fly. Sure, everyone likes to talk about the old Flynn family of bankers. But I have just as many ancestors who chased storms or tried to create flying machines and time-travel contraptions. We Flynns tend to either die young, or grow old and moldy inside a bank, or end up here."

The two of them near an elevator, and Sherwood stops to

press the button for the 4th floor. He hands Caroline the small bouquet of forget-me-nots.

"Ready to meet the most brilliant man I've ever known?" he asks.

Caroline nods hesitantly, without taking her eyes off the bright blue flowers. Each one is marked by a yellow sun in the center of its petals embedded within a delicate white star.

After the elevator rings and slides open its shiny, brass doors, Sherwood and Caroline step into the hallway. Sherwood veers her to the left, and they walk down the hall to room 407. If it weren't for the nurses bustling by in crisp uniforms, or the occasional high-pitched wail or haunted shriek of laughter, it might be easy to simply take this building for an elegant old hotel. But the moment Sherwood opens the door to his grandfather's room, only to see a grizzled old man in pajamas hanging by his knees from a chandelier beneath a tall ceiling, it becomes clear that this facility includes patients that some might term a bit…off kilter.

Sherwood calls out a hello. Immediately, his grandfather swings up and grabs the chandelier with his hands. Then he unravels his legs slowly and manages to release, doing an awkward somersault before falling onto his bed. For a moment, he makes no sound at all, as if he might have gotten the wind knocked out of him. Then he bursts into hoarse laughter and begins wheezing.

"Four!" Sherwood pipes up, holding up four fingers. He

shakes his head. "Oh Grandpa, you used to be able to do at least a double somersault."

The old man is still wheezing too hard in between his choked guffaws to answer.

"Let's see you do better, boy!" he finally spits out.

"Our rating system is one to ten," Sherwood whispers to Caroline. "Kind of like the Olympics."

He sets down his painting and steps over near the bed, climbing onto a small chair poised precariously on top of a wide coffee table before leaping to grab the chandelier. Immediately, Sherwood swings back and forth so hard that the crystals of the chandelier tinkle melodically. To Caroline's shock, Sherwood lets go and flies upwards, tucking his knees tight against his chest and managing to barely do two flips before landing next to his grandfather with a thud. The bed creaks and groans under their weight.

They both start to laugh, making Sherwood's grandfather pound his chest to gasp for struggled breaths.

"Are you next, fine young lady?" Sherwood's grandfather asks Caroline, wheezing again. His breaths strain somewhere between heaves and whistles, making him sound like an old radiator.

Caroline shakes her head, looking petrified.

"There, there now," the grandfather smiles and labors to sit up. "No need to be afraid of our shenanigans. Or anything else in life—right, boy?" He digs an elbow into Sherwood's ribs and points to the canvas he leaned against the wall. "What've you brought for me this time?"

It's at that moment that Caroline appears to recover enough from her jolt to notice the paintings on the walls.

Sherwood's grandfather's room is filled with artwork, similar to what she saw in the gardener's warehouse. Each painting has wild, random swirls of bright colors that spool or angle every which way, often with fragments of wood, metal, or even hay.

"I've got another painting for you, Grandpa," Sherwood says proudly, bolting up from the bed. "I think you're gonna like this one. It's extra special."

"I like all your work," the old man replies gruffly. "Too bad your damn father called it sissy stuff. He wouldn't have been brave enough to paint if his life depended on it—or he might still be here."

Sherwood becomes quiet, studying the grain of the floor for a moment. He steals a glance up at Caroline. "But with this painting, Grandpa, I really outdid myself—"

"That's because you got a girl," his grandfather smirks.

Sherwood can't help blushing and returns his gaze to the floor. But when he swivels the canvas around so his grandfather can see, the old man visibly gasps.

"My God, boy," he says in awe. At first his grandfather scrutinizes the overall shapes and spiraling colors, as though recognizing them as familiar artistic forms. But then he focuses intently on the red eye at the center. His face crinkles into a grin, and he claps his hands, hooting with glee. "What the hell have you done, Sherwood? Tell me all about it!"

Sherwood takes a deep breath, checking Caroline's gaze almost for permission. She gives him a slight smile.

"Well, I heard on the radio the other day that there was a tornado watch, especially in northern Kentucky, so I persuaded Caroline here to help me make the drive."

His grandfather arches his brow in skepticism. "Not anything you haven't done a dozen times before."

"Yeah," Sherwood replies softly, as though still a bit stunned by the experience. "It didn't seem like anything special at first. When we finally saw a funnel touch down, it wasn't that big—barely an F-1 at best, if that. But then, all of a sudden, it shredded a nearby barn and turned toward us. And it *glowed*—"

"Pulsing…" his grandfather nods and drifts off for a moment, as though recalling an old memory. "Like a heart or something, right? Beating within the very core of the twister…"

"Like it was *alive*," Sherwood adds, before swallowing hard. His expression is fiery and intense, still searching for the right way to articulate what he'd witnessed.

"Did it come after you?" his grandfather asks. "Like it somehow *knew* you saw it?"

Sherwood turns to Caroline, whose eyes are wide as saucers now at their shared memory, as if they've stumbled upon something rare and maybe sacred. Sherwood's grandfather gazes right at her, making her nervous.

"It-it picked us up, sir. The wind—" Caroline struggles for the words.

"Yeah. And we were suddenly in the air, dancing with… God," Sherwood finishes.

The old man surprises them both with a big belly laugh, followed by a wheeze.

"You mean the tornado tossed you up and threw you down on your ass!" he bellows, coughing. "You can't fool me, boy! You got lifted, didn't you? Swirled around and planted in the dust!" He slaps his knee with more chuckles. "Believe me—I been there! I saw it once, just like you, and folks say it made me crazy. So insane I left banking to travel the world in search of that red eye again. It's like peering into the heart of God, isn't it?"

Sherwood and Caroline give him hesitant nods.

Sherwood's grandfather slowly rises from his bed and stares at the painting, caressing the gray stubble on his chin. "You know, the first red eye ever recorded within a tornado was in 1881 by John Finley, an early meteorologist. Near as I can tell, the Flynns are the only ones to document it since. I even had a photograph that I captured, but nobody believed it was real." He turns to gaze at Caroline. "Until now."

Caroline blushes and darts her eyes, as though perhaps they're *all* crazy.

"Well, I got a little secret for you," the grandfather says rather sternly. "And I want you to remember it long after I'm gone. You promise?"

Sherwood and Caroline glance at each other with shy approval, then at him.

"It doesn't matter if nobody ever believes you," he continues, "or calls you crazy. The only thing that matters is this: if you really want to get the most out of life, you have to *become what you chase*. So make sure you're chasing something truly wonderful. And in this case, it's pure magic—"

To their surprise, Sherwood's grandfather hobbles slowly over to Caroline and lays his wrinkled hands upon her cheeks. He gazes into her eyes soulfully, as if he can see something of great depth inside her that perhaps she never saw herself. Then he closes his eyes and kisses her on the forehead.

"You'd better hold onto her, boy," he whispers just loud enough for Sherwood to hear. "Because a girl who can see what you see, she's one in a million."

When he removes his fingers from Caroline's face, he takes the forget-me-nots from her hand and turns to shuffle over to the painting, Oddly, he plucks blue petals from the flowers and licks each one, sticking it to the painting with his own spit.

"There," he says, his fingers appearing to tremble with fatigue. "Now you remember what I told you. All right?"

Sherwood and Caroline softly agree.

"And there's something I never mentioned, Sherwood. Which I'm going let you know now."

"W-What's that?" Sherwood asks.

"When I saw that red eye as a young man. The one and only time in my life I got to witness it—well, I was trying to impress a girl, too."

A slight smirk surfaces on Sherwood's cheek.

"Now you two run along, before the nurse comes to enforce lights out. I think she fancies me, you know," Sherwood's grandfather remarks with a gleam in his eye.

Sherwood appears a bit downcast at the thought of having to leave. Even so, he dutifully grabs the painting and tucks it under his arm, motioning for Caroline to head toward the door. Just as he opens it for her, his grandpa calls after him.

"One more thing, Sherwood," he says, his voice sounding thin.

Sherwood swivels around.

"I'm so proud of you."

Sherwood can't hide his big grin this time, though he conceals it quickly by faking a little cough. Beaming, he nods at his grandfather and bids him goodnight, before taking Caroline's hand and giving it a squeeze. They walk down through the hall and return to the shiny, brass doors of the elevator. After the elevator drops them down to the lobby once again, Sherwood and Caroline exit and head back to the front door. They both bow their goodnights to Mr. Barry as he opens the door for them, competing with each other for how fancy they can make their gestures. Then they dash to cross the street and navigate their way in the dark through the Black Woods, back to the gardener's building between Breton and Pinnacle.

"It's getting late," Sherwood whispers, tugging at Caroline's hand to stay in the shadows of the trees. They trot around to the front of the gardener's building as quickly as possible, till they reach the spot where they leave their secret notes in the gaps between the stones.

Sherwood points to a crack where he'll leave his next note.

"Meet me every Wednesday evening, okay? In a different place to keep the administration guessing." He sets down the painting to give her a quick kiss. "I'll find you wherever I've written on the note. It'll be a new place each time, so no one will catch us."

His eyes appear ablaze in the moonlight. "Okay, Caroline?" He glances up at the night sky, then back at her intensely, as if her gaze somehow reflects the constellations. "Two star-lit lovers, till we're old enough to blow this place and spend daylight together."

Sherwood gives her another kiss. Not just any kiss—but a kiss with all the promise he can draw from his soul. "Caroline," he whispers her name like a fragile treasure, "keep coming, please?" He searches her eyes. "Please? Because I think…I-I'm falling—"

Before he can finish, Caroline sweeps him up in a fierce kiss, clutching his face and then running her hands through his hair. Her lips are a storm, working over his, as she backs him up against the wall of the gardner's building, where he braces himself against the stones. All at once, he wraps his long arms around her and picks her up by her thighs, her knees straddling his waist, pouring himself into her.

When Caroline finally breaks away, she sets her feet on the ground and takes a step back, smiling slyly.

"Then I want that painting, Mr. Flynn," she insists, pointing at the canvas he'd dropped as they kissed. "Because it has your heart."

Without another word, Caroline picks up the canvas and begins walking confidently back to Pinnacle, as though she holds the whole world under her arm.

And Sherwood is left gasping, his eyes following the moonlit trail of her steps.

"Meet you Wednesday!" Caroline raises her hand to the stars and throws him a cocky wave. Ever so briefly, she swivels around to give him a wink.

And Sherwood extends a silly bow to her, laughing.

He turns to dart away faster than a flitting shadow, disappearing into the night as the bells of Pinnacle and Breton ring their first warnings for impending lights out.

But what Sherwood doesn't see is the boy who steps out from the tree shadows nearby. He glares at Sherwood for a moment, then turns to stare longingly at the beautiful young woman who carries a canvas as she walks back to Pinnacle. His eyes trace her every curve, the sway of her hips and bounce of her steps, with a kind of yearning that borders somewhere between obsession and a piercing desire that teeters on hatred. In the moonlight that filters through the trees, the white script on the back of his varsity jacket illuminates the letters of his last name:

HELMS.

15

The stone grows cold beneath my hand again, feeling like ice between my fingers. As cold as that strange look I saw on that boy's face in the shadows—warm one moment, and chilling the next.

I stare at Creek, only to see something in his eyes that frightens me more.

Undiluted rage—

"Helms… *Bradford…Helms*," he hisses in a way that sends goosebumps charging all over my body. "My goddamn stepdad! He did something to them after that, didn't he? Out of jealousy—"

Before I can take a breath, Creek's slamming his fist against the filing cabinet over and over, kicking at it and punching till it collapses into a warped heap on the floor, spilling all the files. He's a bloody mess now, just like he was in our wagon, and I feel as though I'm caught inside one of his terrifying nightmares.

"Why don't you talk to me!" he hollers to the rafters as if he's screaming at a ghost. "We know you're around here somewhere, haunting these schools! Why don't you show us where you are, Caroline? Be done with it and tell us what he did! Go ahead, I dare you to hurt *me* like you've been hurting those other people! Just lead us to Bradford Helms—"

Creek topples over a desk and another filing cabinet, scattering things around the room and slamming his fists and boots into whatever he can find. He's a whirlwind of anger, his strikes and kicks turning into a blur.

"Creek! Stop it!" I cry. "You're making too much noise. Someone's going to catch us—"

At that moment, all my fears are confirmed by the sound of a shrill siren outside. Yet strangely, loose leaves charge past the window at break-neck speeds, followed by twigs and small branches. Without warning, the windowpane bursts, sending glass shards all over the floor. My scream matches the wail of sirens outside.

It's then that I realize the sirens aren't police—they're tornado warnings.

The ferocious wind swirls into the office room and sends files flying. Sherwood's file, which lies at my feet, loses several pages that spiral in air. I leap to grab them, and to my shock, I notice one of the pages is on Pinnacle letterhead—in Mother Superior's handwriting.

It's addressed to the Breton headmaster...

"Creek!" I gasp, trembling. "She—she must've known something!"

"Who? Known what?" Creek whips around, chest still heaving from his rampage. It doesn't appear to bother him that his arms are trickling with blood. Clearly, he no longer cares who might find his DNA—or that it might also match Sherwood Flynn's.

"This is a letter from Mother Superior!" I hold it up to show him. "She must have known what happened to them—"

Clearing my throat, I read her words aloud:

Dear Headmaster Thompson,

Although Sherwood Alastair Flynn V is now deceased, Caroline Gust has confidentially admitted to me that he was, in fact, the father of her unborn child. I write this letter to you with deep regret that the security procedures at Pinnacle were unable to prevent their union. However, it must be noted that Mr. Flynn had a history of ingeniously breaking the rules at Breton regarding his persistent truancy. Fortunately, Ms. Gust has chosen to leave our boarding school system of her own free will, and I have convinced her not to press charges against the eminent Flynn family, given her own responsibility in their indiscretions. I assure you, Mr. Thompson, that her file has been expunged from our system, and she will never be spoken of or referred to within our halls again. There is no need to inform the Flynn family of her existence, nor that of her child, so that the good name of the Flynns and Breton Boarding School for Boys will not be marred in any way. Please accept my apologies regarding this turn of events, and may God bless you and your inspired leadership at Breton.

— MOTHER SUPERIOR

The second I finish reading her letter, the paper flies out of my hand. The wind outside is so fierce it's lashing my hair against my face, making my heart race. The warning sirens are deafening now, and I'm terrified we're about to be goners—

I dash to grab Mother Superior's letter that slapped against a window pane, stuffing it into my pocket, when I spy a funnel in the distance, just as the Stone of Thieves begins to flash in my hand.

"Creek!" I cry, "we've gotta find low-lying shelter —NOW!"

Creek is staring out the window at a tornado on the moonlit horizon as though numb. We're at the top of a hill in Cincinnati here at Breton, where under the full moon's glare we can barely make out a long thin funnel, like a twisted broomstick, sweeping its way through the sleepy valley. Sprays of debris fly up into the sky while the funnel works its way erratically toward the Ohio River. In total calm, Creek's gaze travels to the stone in my hand, which is pulsing scarlet within the star-like cracks of the heart. Gone is Creek's rage for a moment. It's been replaced by an eerie stillness that sends chills chasing through me. He's utterly emotionless, his ice-blue eyes fixated on the sky.

"You're right," he says quietly, ignoring the heavier branches that fly into the room now, mesmerized by the spiraling force maybe only twenty miles away. "We have to get out of here."

His bloody glove clasps my hand to lead me back down the dark hallway, but he doesn't seem in a hurry. Impatient, I tug at him furiously, and as soon as we make it to the stairwell, I drag him to charge with me down the steps.

When we reach the ground floor, I naturally expect Creek to keep going to the basement. But instead, he creaks open the outside door and orders me to head downstairs. Then he gives me a quick, goodbye kiss before he darts outside.

Straight into the storm—

"What the hell are you doing?" I cry, chasing after him and yanking on his flannel shirt as hard as I can. "Are you out of your mind? We have to get back inside—"

Under a streetlamp, I see Creek's eyes flash—crazy, just like Sherwood's were on that night he set up his canvas in the path of the twister. All at once, he's someone I don't know, made of pure wildness, an untamed force inside him as powerful and unpredictable as the funnel that's steadily climbing up the hill. He grabs me by the shoulders, his leather gloves bloodying my flannel shirt.

"No—go back, Robin! To the basement!!" he shouts over the wind's roar. "I have to do this! You have to let me!"

I shake my head, confused, barely able to see him through the strands of hair that whip against my face. "But you could *die* out there, Creek!" I cry, nearly hysterical. "Come with me, now—"

"Robin, if I dare to look at the heart," he cups my face and kisses me, shouting into my ear, "I'll not only find out what happened to them—I might see their very souls."

I hold up the Stone of Thieves to Creek, which glows crimson between my clenched fingers now, my whole body shaking. "All right!" I relent. "But we can do this safer in the basement of the building—"

"No!" Creek interrupts, placing his palm over the stone in my hand and shaking his head. "Not this heart." He points to the crooked funnel that blasts past a moonlit building in the distance. "*That one*—"

When I glance toward it, what I see knocks the breath out of me.

Pulsing, within the core of the funnel only about fifteen miles away, is an eerie column of crimson light, iridescent, and surrounded by billows of smoky, swirling debris. The illumination appears to throb, just like a beating heart.

"You said you wanted me whole, Robin!" Creek hollers. "Well I'm here, right now, exactly where they were, once! And for maybe the only time in my life, I have the chance to see what my mom—and my *real* dad—actually saw."

He kisses me with everything he's got. His lips are locked on mine and his whole being pours into me in that moment, as though he's reached a crossroads and is about to face something that will either bring us closer together, or tear us apart forever.

"You have to let me go, Robin!" he says finally, breaking away. "*You* dared to go inside the Stone of Thieves once to find the real soul of your mother, remember?"

Shivering in terror, I recall how dangerous that really was, and my eyes meet Creek's.

"Well now *I'm* going to face that heart to see the souls of my parents. When I'm done, Robin, nothing will be the same. *We* won't be the same. But I'll have finally seen it—and isn't that what you really wanted?"

I duck my head against his chest in tears, hugging him with all my might.

Of course that's what I wanted! For Creek to find the missing pieces of his parents and lay their ghosts to rest. To heal inside. Despite my heart trying to pound straight out of my chest, I grit my teeth and nod against his shoulder.

I'm totally speechless. This is mad—

Yet something deep inside me knows I can't, and won't, stop him.

How could I deny an orphaned and abused young man, who I love beyond my own life, and who *never* got the chance to meet his own father, the opportunity to see the very thing that Sherwood Flynn lived for?

"You're going to the basement—now!!" Creek insists.

With that, he hoists me into his arms, cradling my head tight against his hard chest. He carries me boldly, racing through the storm and dodging thick chunks of hedges that barrel our way. When we reach the Breton building, he flings open the door and sets me to my feet.

"Stay here! Promise me!" Creek cries, his blue eyes fierce in their protective urge. "Because Robin, I'd kill myself if something ever happened to you—"

"Okay!" I reply, nodding.

With my fingers crossed…

Because off all people in the world, Creek ought to know by now that I'm a veteran liar.

One of the very best—

So of course I step through that door and bolt down the dark stairwell till Creek can't see me anymore. But the second he returns to the storm, I'm back up to the doorway in a shot.

"This is insane!" I burst, my voice stolen by the wind. I watch helplessly as Creek strides onto the grounds that separate Breton and Pinnacle, into the Black Woods. He simply stands and stares at the furious red column within the dark whirl that's coming his way. It takes all the strength I have within me not to dash out there and join him, not to interrupt this sacred moment and let him do what's in his heart. Yet I'm terrified at the sight of the oncoming funnel, which heaves in and out as it gains power like a giant bellows. Trees and fences lift in its wake, spinning in the air and dropping to the ground like children's toys. Breton and Pinnacle are dark and utterly lifeless now, as most of the students and faculty have the good sense to hit the basements. Heart hammering, I raise the Stone of Thieves high in my hand and whisper a prayer, begging for Creek's safety. As the core of the twister radiates through the ruby stone, almost as though they're both pulsing and speaking to me, the wind howls over the steady whine of the sirens' blares.

And in a flash, Sherwood and Caroline are once again standing right in front of me. Only they aren't at the gardener's building anymore. They're at another building near Pinnacle, the one that stores extra student desks and chairs. It's still night time, but the wind is gone, replaced by stars that twinkle above them on a balmy spring night like their shining hopes.

And Caroline is giggling.

She covers her mouth and holds up a crumpled note to Sherwood that she'd found, which features his handwriting.

"Be there or be square?" she laughs, pointing to a cartoon he drew of himself unhappily locked inside a three-dimensional cube. "Don't you think that's a bit nerdy?"

Sherwood steals a kiss, his eyes flashing the same way Creek's did in front of the storm. "Well it did the trick, didn't it?" He laughs. "You're here."

Caroline shrugs with a smirk. But then his sudden shift of expression startles her a little.

"I have a crazy idea," Sherwood whispers. "Well, at least, it might sound a little crazy——"

"You're *not* crazy," Caroline says quietly. She loops a stray lock of hair from his eyes and swipes a kiss of her own. "You just never forgot to see the world in all its color." She pauses, gazing at her shoes for a second. Her eyes become tender. "You brought back the color to my life too, you know. And frankly, I think there's something pretty sane about that."

"Maybe," he nods, "but just wait till you hear my idea." Sherwood inhales a deep breath, biting his lip as though more nervous than usual. He places both hands on Caroline's shoulders and stares into her eyes. "Let's stop hiding, Caroline. I mean it——we've been meeting at night like this for weeks. Always stuffing notes for our next rendezvous into these stones. Let's run away together. Tomorrow, for good. You and me."

Caroline rolls her eyes. "I don't have a dime, Sherwood. Or a place to go, or steady meals. You talk about our schools being prisons. But at least they give a scholarship chick like me a warm bed. It's better than being farmed out to the foster system."

"I do." Sherwood runs his fingers through her long, wayward locks that tend to fall into her eyes. "I *do* have money, Caroline. I turned eighteen today——"

"What? Happy birthday!" she bursts, surprised. "You didn't tell me your——"

"That's not the point," Sherwood sighs, shaking his head. "I've got a trust fund, Caroline. That my mom can't control. It's handled by a conservator at one of our banks and it kicked in today. We could go where no one will find us or call us crazy ever again. I can sell my art——you can help me create it. We could be S & C Studios. And there's not a damn thing my mother can do. She doesn't care anyway—as long as I'm not in her hair."

Caroline gazes at him with a familiar sadness in her eyes, tinged with regret.

"Oh Sherwood, you're hardly the first boy who finds me beautiful. I know what it's like to be discarded. I amuse you for now—I'm your new toy. But as soon as a new storm or another thrill comes along—"

Sherwood crushes his lips against hers.

"Marry me, Caroline! I'm different! I see the beauty and wildness in you, right here! Right now!" He taps her heart. "Please go on this magic carpet ride with me. What have we got to lose? If we're legally married when you turn eighteen, then all the money I have will be yours. There's not a damn thing anyone can do about it."

Caroline searches his eyes—they are a blue fire.

"I'm just afraid of being your...dream girl," she confesses. "Someone two-dimensional that works better for you on some canvas than in real life."

Sherwood stands iron straight. His lop-sided grin has vanished, along with the twinkle in his eye. He's no longer the crafty magician who makes everything seem more exciting and glamorous than perhaps it really is.

Once again, he's back to being that boy with the searing gaze who scares girls from the shadows.

"Caroline," he says gravely, "this *is* real life. *Your* life. And you might not want to admit it, but somehow, somewhere, somebody's always taken care of you and told you what to do. Either your grandma, or Pinnacle, or Dr. Cutler. They've called the shots and you stepped in line. I'm a *choice*, dammit! I can't guarantee things will be perfect. But I can tell you it will be real. Full of highs and lows and storms that are glorious one minute and terrifying the next. I love you, Caroline, and I want to create a future with you. Who knows how it's gonna turn out? We could go broke and live on the streets for all I know. But something tells me we'll still chase storms and wild things."

Sherwood tenderly brushes his fingers against her cheek. "And we'll be together. It's up to you, Caroline. But I want you to know, tomorrow, I'm getting the hell out of here."

Caroline gasps like he'd slapped her with those words.

She stares into his eyes, at the finality of his decision that's clearly marked by his intense gaze. Drawing in a deep breath, she lifts her eyes to the stars.

"I don't want to stay here without you."

"Not good enough," Sherwood shakes his head. His hands cup her cheeks, making her flinch. "Do you love me, Caroline? It's okay to say no. Totally okay. Because I can't paint a future with the two of us in it if you don't."

Caroline's lips slide into a sly grin and her eyes begin to sparkle.

"Are you *kidding* me, Sherwood Flynn?"

She dives for a kiss and links her arms around his neck. "Don't you know I'm totally crazy about you?" she says, breathless. For a few seconds she stares at her old boarding school, as if bidding it goodbye, and nods. "I fell in love with you the first moment I saw you, Sherwood. That amazing boy who slips in and out of shadows and shows people how to see what's real—even if he has to scare them sometimes to do it.

You're an artist to the core—and you found my heart." She places her hand gently on his chest, feeling the throb of his heartbeat. "So let's get the hell out of here tomorrow and start painting our dreams."

Sherwood's smile stretches as wide as the Ohio River. He lifts her in his arms and kisses her so hard that when they finally break away, their chests are heaving. He points across the school grounds to the gardener's building.

"Tomorrow, sneak out of your dorm after lights out. I'll let you know with a note stuffed between the stones where I'll meet you with a car." He smirks a little. "It'll be borrowed, of course. But we can return it later. Make sure you have a duffle bag with all your stuff, and your grandma's picture. Because once we do this, Caroline, there's no going back."

"You're really going to meet me, at ten o'clock sharp?" Caroline replies a bit nervously. "'Cause I don't want loiter near the Black Woods between Breton and Pinnacle after lights out unless you're on time. I've heard stories about those Breton boys—what they sometimes do to girls."

"I *won't be* a Breton boy anymore," Sherwood laughs, pulling her in for a kiss. "And don't worry, I'll protect you. We'll meet on time, just like always, Caroline. Except I'll have a suitcase in my hand—and a car."

He kisses her again and again. When he stops, he gazes into her eyes as though he wants to remember her delicate features under the starlight forever.

"You can count on me," Sherwood whispers. "Remember, Caroline? I keep my promises."

❧ 16 ❧

As Sherwood and Caroline begin to fade and slip from my sight, the twister's so close now that I know I have to dive for cover, or I'll surely die.

But my impulse to rescue Creek overrides any natural survival instinct. I can't stop my feet from tearing straight into the storm, just like he did.

And into the path of the oncoming funnel.

"Creek!!" I shriek, grabbing him and tugging with all my might. My sights are across the grounds at Pinnacle, on a door I see nearby beneath a streetlamp in an office building with a tall tower. Above the tower flies the black Pinnacle Pride flag, set off by floodlights. Never mind the fact that we used to joke this building contains Mother Superior's instruments of torture. As long as it has a basement, it'll do—and we don't have time to waste. "C'mon! We have to GO!!"

Thank God he finally listens to me! We race as fast as we

can, feeling as if we're running through deep water from the force of wind and sheets of rain that now pelt us.

Except, all of a sudden, I realize it's not *we* anymore—

It's just *me*...

Creek's standing before the storm in the wavering glow of a streetlamp with his arms outstretched, as if inviting—no, *daring*—the tornado to strike him. He's not the least bit afraid, and he stares at the pulsing red core of the funnel with an oddly peaceful expression, almost as though he *knows* it. Knows its wild quirks and personality, its erratic momentum and fierce language of power. Then he tilts his head slightly, as if listening, and lets his eyes fall closed. His arms are wide open, welcoming the twister like a long-lost relative that he fully intends to embrace. All at once, the wind lifts his feet, and before I know it, he's rising in the air like a ghost.

Petrified, I dash over to grab at Creek's legs, wondering if he's somehow become possessed. Has the ghost of Pinnacle overcome his very soul? Fortunately, I manage to hang onto him by his boots and pull him down with everything I've got, even though I fear my weight is hardly enough for ballast.

"Creek!" I cry, with visions of losing him to Oz. "Don't leave me!"

Creek turns slowly to gaze at me, like I'd called him down from heaven. His face is as still as a stone, as though he'd seen God.

And in that moment, his blue eyes appear as distant as a stranger, and somehow frighteningly old. Yet when he lowers his arms, our feet fall and strike the ground, where we land together in a heap. Strangely enough, the wind feels like it's starting to die down now, and the funnel has begun to lose its color and shape, becoming merely thin wisps of clouds that swirl like loose scarves. Still panicked, I dig my fingers into Creek's arm and haul him with all my strength to the side door of the Pinnacle building. Swinging it open, I gasp in relief when we reach an elevator that leads to all floors. I mash the "B" button for the basement with my fist as soon as the doors open, and we step inside. But instead of going down to the bottom floor, the elevator begins to rise.

Nothing alters its course—not pounding for other floors or beating on the emergency button. Despite my furious hits, the elevator remains eerily quiet, insulated from the sounds outside as it rises higher and higher. At this point, I have to wonder if we are, in fact, the next victims of Pinnacle's resident ghost—

What's more, the elevator appears to be racing at high speed.

All the way to the top of the stone tower.

When it finally slows its bullet pace and stops with a jolt, we can't manage to pry open the doors. They're shut as tight as a prison cell.

"Caroline!" I shout desperately.

This time, *I'm* the one who's angry—

"Why are you doing this?" I demand. "Sherwood loved you! And Creek loves you, in spite of what happened—I know he does! Why else would he have experienced such pain when you died, and risked his life in this storm? He wanted to know what happened to you two!"

As if responding to my outburst, all lights in the elevator flicker for a few moments and turn off, spooking the life out of me. Yet slowly, the elevator doors creak open as though invisible hands pull them aside. Before us is a lush, dark hallway lit only by the dancing flames of creepy, wall-mounted torches. It's so haunting and gothic, it's enough to send most people running away screaming. As my eyes adjust to the light, I notice the hallway is filled with medieval tapestries, gilded paintings—even a knight's suit of armor that glints in the torch lights.

Holding my breath, I tremble as we step out. But Creek strides boldly to the metal shell of the knight and rips the axe right out of its hand. Its armored fingers clatter to the floor, leaving a hollow echo. My first impulse is to turn around and pound on the elevator button to go down again, but it's futile. The elevator doors have sealed tight as a vise, leaving us stranded here. Swallowing hard, that's when I realize the sirens have stopped. Through a small window in the hallway, I see the twinkling lights across the city of Cincinnati. Directly below us, people are hesitantly stepping out of their homes into the light of the street lamps. They appear exhausted and relieved at the same time that more damage wasn't done. There are toppled trees and a few cars left on their sides. But otherwise, from what I can tell in the glow of the street lights, no buildings were demolished. Not even a twig or stray leaf blows across the window anymore.

The storm has passed.

"That elevator's not going to let us back down anytime soon, baby," Creek says. He clutches my hand to keep me from mashing the button again. "Someone—or *something*—wants us to be here."

I whip the Stone of Thieves from my pocket and hold it up by its chain, hoping for guidance, but it's gone cold.

If ever a place feels haunted, this is it.

Scratches grate against the window pane behind me, making me jump.

It's a dove—

The bird flaps and taps its beak insistently on the glass. I pry open the small window, watching it dart in. It flitters to the head of the armored knight and hesitates for a moment, then coos softly and sails down the hall.

Dare we follow? Could this be Caroline's friend and only confidant, Bright Eyes?

Or perhaps Caroline herself...

All along the hallway are more medieval artifacts that look expensive, if not priceless, like everyone at Pinnacle suspected. But instead of being instruments of torture, they're stunning artworks in their detail and craftsmanship. Tryptych paintings of biblical scenes accented in gold leaf, stone sculptures that look like they once adorned European cathedrals, more elegantly woven tapestries—they're extraordinary beyond belief.

Yet the dove ignores them all and flies through a doorway at the end of the short hall.

From where we stand, I can tell there's a light on and a big desk in the office room along with a file cabinet wedged into a corner. We know Caroline's records were destroyed when she left Pinnacle. What could this bird be leading us to? I hold up the stone, secretly hoping it might remain cloudy and offer us an excuse to leave. But dammit, it's becoming as bright as a stoplight now, making me feel as though the dove knows something we don't. Despite my fears that a ghost could pop out at any moment from inside a painting or suit of armor, I press forward down the hallway with Creek and his axe by my side.

Finally, as we step inside the room, it's confirmed that this is Mother Superior's notorious tower office by the certificates and awards on the walls that bear her title. Alongside them are lists of the most notorious leaders of her Pinnacle Patrol, etched on plaques in brass, and the dates they graduated. Yet curiously, a newspaper article is taped to the wall next to the plaques with a headline that reads, *Top Pinnacle Pride Alumni Die Mysteriously This Spring: Drew Ball & Gwynn Sterling, along with Student Skyler Worth. Accidents or Haunting?*

The stark, black boldness of the caption gives me the shivers. And even though I'm no longer a student here, the very thought of being in this room makes my stomach turn. Here is where Mother Superior, nicknamed "The Enforcer" and "Darth Vader", banished derelict girls from Pinnacle for good, ruining their reputations in Cincinnati high society if the mood struck her. And she was the one who knew of my mother's liaison with my father all those years ago. It was her snitching that led to my mother's miserable years of incarceration by the hand of her corrupt family in a rural Italian convent, where my mother had been left to rot. Girls' lives could be promoted or destroyed by Mother Superior's whims, which she wielded like a sword with relish.

And I have to admit, I'm *still* scared of her.

The last time I saw her, she knocked me upside the head with her mahogany cane and demanded the Stone of Thieves.

Why? Did she really need to be a penny richer, or to collect more precious treasures for her tower?

I don't know. Darting my eyes back and forth, I muster the

courage to step past the transom into her office, hoping the ruby heart can show us quickly where to go, so we can get the hell out of here.

Yet the second I do, the door slams shut behind us, giving me a fright.

And before I can blink, Creek's axe is upon the neck of none other than Mother Superior, pinning her to a wall.

She's in her long black habit, like usual—all six feet of her.

And the only problem is, she's got a pearl-handled pistol in her hand.

Pointing at Creek's forehead.

"Give me the stone," she says with a chilling vehemence that reminds me this is no imposter. That ashen face and crook nose are the real thing, along with her beady black eyes that are enough to scare the crap out of most any living creature.

And to my shock, I see her holding Sherwood Flynn's last painting beneath her arm—

The one depicting the red eye of the storm.

She must've known we were coming…

Did she spot us outside? Or was she tipped off by the presence of Bright Eyes on a windowsill? How could she know we might want that painting?

"Go ahead, try it," Creek growls to her in defiance, wedging the axe tighter against her neck. "Your throat will be sliced in two before you can even finish pulling that trigger. You ready to meet your maker tonight? 'Cause I sure as hell am happy take you with me—"

Never before have I seen the formidable Mother Superior actually flinch. Yet she has a stubborn, white-knuckled grip on that painting as if her life depends on it.

"Trade!" she cries out, desperately searching my eyes for some sign of concession. "The painting for the stone! We sold the others for a small fortune. This is the last one I have. It's worth thousands—"

"How'd you know we'd want Sherwood Flynn's painting?" I spit back at her, glancing at Creek. "Tell us what you know!"

I dig for her crumpled letter to the Breton Headmaster in my pocket and hold it up, proving that I recognize she's aware of what happened to Sherwood and Caroline.

"The stone knows!" Mother Superior seethes, her eyes flickering. "It knows everything!"

Her free hand is reaching out like a crazed woman, clawing her fingers toward me—this woman who has all the wealth a person could crave, and apparently a fortune from Sherwood's paintings, too. Yet it's then that I notice the PP ring from her finger is gone.

She *always* wore that ring! It was her shield—a reminder to everyone of the power she wielded through her minions at the school. Why on earth would she remove it—was she afraid of Caroline's ghost as well?

"Tell us what happened to Caroline!" I demand holding up the stone to her like a spooky amulet. "Or I'll give Creek the signal to slice your throat!"

And God as my witness, I mean it. We know where to dump bodies at Bender Lake, and I'm sick to death of the way this woman has destroyed so many lives—and nearly destroyed mine. Yet to my astonishment, I see Creek's hold relax.

It's only then that I notice Mother Superior's hand is trembling so hard on her pistol that she wouldn't have a prayer of shooting Creek, even if she wanted to. In her eyes is something I've never seen before—

Pure terror...

Yet it isn't focused on me. Or Creek. Or even the thought of...death.

It's more like a fear of remaining *alive*.

Lips pursed, Mother Superior thrusts her neck up tighter against the blade of the axe, so that it creases a heavy line against her pale, crinkled skin, as though daring Creek to end her life.

And I glance at the ruby heart in my hand, which radiates fiercely between my fingers, growing hotter by the second and pulsing like a morse code. I stare back at Mother Superior.

"Don't kill her, Creek—that's what she wants!" I cry, putting the pieces together of her completely bizarre behavior. The stone *does* know something—and whatever it is will surely damn her.

Quick as a flash, Creek seizes her gun and tosses it into a fish tank in a corner of the room. As the gun sinks to the bottom, the angel fish skitter to the edge of the glass.

"Start talking," Creek hisses.

"Just let me touch it!" Mother Superior screams as the dove wings to another side of the office. It lands on a marble statue of Saint Francis of Assisi in the corner, holding a bird on his outstretched hand, the same size as the dove.

Cooing repeatedly, the dove taps at the statue, till I notice the marble bird has a line across its belly.

Like it's a secret container...

I dash over to the statue and lift the head of the marble bird. The ruby heart has become a beacon in my hand, so hot

I have to set it down on a nearby file cabinet. Inside the bird, I discover a small, yellowed note.

"No!" Mother Superior recoils as I pick up the piece of paper. Swiftly, I read aloud its cryptic message:

Meet me at the Pinnacle front gate.
Tonight, we start our forever.
I love you.

— *SHERWOOD*

I begin to tremble, goosebumps running down my body, and I have to lean onto the statue for support. Hot tears sting the corners of my eyes.

"Y-you *stole* Sherwood's last note to Caroline?" I gasp. "On the night they were going to run away?"

I shoot a glance at Creek to see if he understands what I'm talking about. He nods at me with a sad knowing in his eyes—he must've somehow seen the same vision I did.

"It was for their safety!" Mother Superior replies, clasping her hands to hide where the ring is missing from her finger. "Who knows what kind of trouble they could've gotten into! Caroline was pregnant by then, though she hadn't told him. So when that Helms boy tipped me off, I never dreamed my PP girls would…"

"Would what?" Creek bursts, dropping his axe and grabbing her by the shoulders. He glares into her eyes as if he wants to set her body on fire. "What did Bradford Helms and your PP girls do after they found the note?" he demands, shaking her. "Tell me what happened to Sherwood and Caroline!"

Mother Superior throws her hulking shoulder against Creek, all two hundred-plus pounds of her, and strikes him against the head, knocking him backwards for a second. She lunges for the fish tank, grabbing the wet pistol and holding it to her own temple, clicking on the trigger over and over like a madwoman. Creek simply lets her follow through on her pathetic gesture, shaking his head.

"Death won't do you a favor now," he says, ripping the pistol from her hand. "You can't hide anymore."

Yet true to form, Mother Superior hardly looks beaten. Despite her bulk, to my surprise, she knocks over a chair and bolts for the window like she intends to jump—

And all I have to do is shove the marble statue of Saint Francis in front of her, blocking her path.

Just as quickly, Creek barricades the office door with his body so she has nowhere to go.

"No!" she cries in agony like a trapped animal, tearing at the fabric of her habit at the edges of her cheeks.

Wild-eyed, she swivels around, chest heaving, but there are no more escape routes. Her eyes have become mesmerized by the stone, glimmering on the file cabinet, and she dashes over to try and grab it—

Creek beats her and seizes the ruby heart with his sleeve, his long arms holding it higher than she can reach.

Mother Superior whimpers and falls to the floor. In a heap, she begins rocking back and forth like a child, sobbing.

And there's a part of me that wants to haul off and kick

her right now. Beat her while she's down like she did to so many others. But Creek grabs my shoulder and pulls me back.

Before I can protest, he crouches beside Mother Superior. Rather than hurt her in any way, he sets the ruby heart inside a pewter goblet on her desk and cradles her sad, sagging face.

"It's over," he says softly. "The past caught up with you. Isn't it time to tell the truth? Sherwood was my dad—but you already guessed that, didn't you? I must look a lot like him. After Bradford Helms stole his last note to Caroline and gave it you, what did you order your PP girls to do?"

"I never told them to do that!" she screeches, trembling. "They got out of control. I didn't know what the PP were really capable of in those woods—"

"What woods?" I pipe up. "The Black Woods between Pinnacle and Breton?"

Mother Superior nods, but her face is still shielded from me.

And before I know it, she's reached up to her desk to swipe the Stone of Thieves from the goblet with her bare hands, in spite of its incendiary heat. Stunned, Creek and I grasp her shoulders, horrified as blisters instantly form on her stubborn, thick fingers. Nevertheless, her hand tightens over the ruby heart with a death grip—

And all at once, we are there.

Watching on that dark night when Sherwood stood before the front gate of Pinnacle. He's under a streetlamp with a stolen car idling, waiting for Caroline…

Sherwood's Breton uniform is gone. He's wearing an old flannel shirt, a lot like Creek's, and torn, faded jeans. Time and time again he checks his wristwatch and sighs, to no avail.

Then, like shadows seeping from the huge oak trees that flank the Pinnacle wrought-iron fence, several figures edge toward him. Sherwood hears the rustle of leaves beneath their sneakers and turns around.

A burly teenager hops over the convertible car door to seat himself behind the wheel.

It's Bradford Helms.

"White Impala? Pretty slick, Sherwood. Ready for a drive?"

"Where's Caroline?" Sherwood bursts, his fists tight. "What did you do with her—"

"Nothing you haven't done already," Bradford smirks.

It's then that Sherwood's face registers that Bradford has been watching them all along...*stalking* them.

"You didn't really think you could bang the most beautiful girl in Cincinnati without the rest of us taking a turn, did you, Sherwood? Finders keepers, losers weepers, asshole."

The shock that riddles through Sherwood, as he turns in the direction of the gardener's warehouse in the Black Woods, freezes him in place. But then lightning appears to snap inside his veins as he throws Bradford a vicious punch to the face. He swiftly vaults over the fence in front of Pinnacle and bolts for the trees.

"Caroline!!" Sherwood cries, legs drumming as fast as he can make them. "Caroline! Hold on, I'm coming—"

He is a blur—something almost supernatural overtakes him, eyes blazing and limbs whipping forward as he covers the ground toward the Black Woods with huge strides. Yet within seconds, it proves not to be enough. Bradford and his friends leap the fence and charge after him, their thick varsity-trained legs overtaking him on the Pinnacle front lawn. There are four of them, and they laugh while trading turns mashing his body like a punching bag.

Impossibly, Sherwood stumbles to his feet, taking fist after fist to his head and gut as though he were made of iron. His sheer will, though he's bloody and spitting out teeth, startles them as he lunges for Bradford and clutches his throat, twisting at his windpipe with every ounce of strength he has left. "Bring me Caroline!" he chokes through a garble of blood and spit. "Or I'll kill you! NOW—"

Despite the fact that the boys have all jumped him, knocking him to the ground, Sherwood takes Bradford down with him. Bradford's face appears nearly blue in the glow of the moonlight and his fists begin to go limp as Sherwood holds him by the throat as tenaciously as a pitbull. But when his friends kick Sherwood in the face, knocking him to the grass like a lifeless puppet, Bradford hesitantly blinks. He slowly sits up, dizzied, and swivels his chin left and right. Then he stares blankly at Sherwood.

"Th-throw him in the car," he manages to sputter before clutching at the grass and struggling to his knees. Before long he's on his feet, wobbly, but standing. "We'll take this f-fucker on his last joy ride—"

The other boys simply laugh. Yet when they turn to grab Sherwood's limbs, he's already gone.

He'd suckered them by playing possum.

Barely conscious, Sherwood weaves back and forth in the darkness of the trees, slipping into shadows. Bradford orders his friends to fan out, but Sherwood has already climbed into the canopy of a large oak, waiting for his moment.

"Go back and take your turns with Caroline!" Bradford laughs savagely. "That'll flush him out. The PP girls have it all arranged. Drew Ball and Gwynn Sterling told her Sherwood dumped her, and they have her behind the big maple tree, ready and waiting."

"No!! Caroline!" Sherwood cries, dropping from the tree. He knows he's taking the bait, but with a searing focus he dashes like a man on fire. Bradford's mob easily tackles him anyway, kicking at him until he's rendered nearly senseless. Yet something within Sherwood refuses to let his eyes fall closed. He stares, unblinking, his gaze as blood-red and intense as the center of the tornado he once painted, into the direction of the gardener's warehouse. With his last, hoarse breaths, he reaches out toward the darkness of the Black Woods as if he might be able touch Caroline's soul.

"I…love…you…" he whispers.

Sherwood's lips move slowly to form the words, before his head slumps to the grass. He grips a delicate patch of blue wildflowers, as though trying to hold onto life, crushing them in his fingers until his hand falls slack.

"Never…forget…"

❧ 18 ❧

Mother Superior howls and drops the ruby heart to the floor. Furiously, she blows on her palms that have become a blistered and bloody mess as she startles back to reality. Her eyes are frantic, desperately searching the smoke that the stone makes as it singes the wooden planks, as though it were a magical incense capable of prophecy. Shaking her head, she mumbles over and over with the intensity of a prayer.

"Help me!" she begs the Stone of Thieves. "Please, please help—"

Creek studies the charred outline of a heart that the stone burns into the floor. He takes Mother Superior's wounded hands in his. "Tell us now," he says firmly. "What did they do with Sherwood?"

Mother Superior gazes at him, her coal-black eyes heavy-laden with grief. "B-Bradford and his friends loaded Sherwood's body in the car," she confesses. "They deliberately crashed it into a tree on the passenger side to make it look like an accident. Th-They let it burn—"

"Burn?" Creek presses. He is a wall of strength, despite the horror of her words that rattle me to the core. "You mean they *incinerated* him?"

Mother Superior's crying too hard now to speak. At last, she gasps for breath and manages to spit out more. "I-I didn't know how much Bradford obsessed about winning Caroline, h-how far he'd go. My two top Pinnacle Pride girls —the ones the ghost killed—they told her Sherwood dumped her because he found out she was pregnant, and he was never coming back. It was all a lie! Then the girls escorted her to the Black Woods, where Bradford's other friends…"

"Raped her?" I choke, tears running down my throat.

Mother Superior struggles to nod.

"She d-didn't know Bradford was behind it all. I guess he'd do anything to call Caroline his own—even break her, if that's what it took. He told her afterwards that Sherwood was two-faced liar who never loved her, and who'd ditched her and got what he deserved. Then he convinced her he was the only one who'd take care of her."

"But you and your girls made sure she was expelled from Pinnacle, didn't you? A pregnant, underage girl! All alone! How could you?"

"It was a mistake!" Mother Superior buries her head into her tortured hands that are oozing with blood. "I was in too deep to get out anymore! There's got to be a way to change it, to appease her ghost. Just let me go back in t—"

A cuckoo clock on the wall strikes against the hour. A little door whips open, releasing a tiny bird that sends out a loud call.

"Time..." Creek whispers, nodding. He gazes at the pulsing stone on the floor. "That's it—"

He glances at the cuckoo bird and back at the smoking ruby heart.

"You were never after the riches the legend says the stone brings, were you? All along, you wanted it to help you go back in—"

"Time?" I finish for him, utterly shocked. "Oh my God—you actually thought you could *change* what happened?"

I'm not sure Mother Superior can hear me anymore. She's crossing herself and repeating Hail Marys, rocking as she shakes her head. She appears crazy now—a broken woman so riddled with guilt that she's lost any hold on reality. When I see the lights flicker on in the surrounding buildings of Pinnacle and Breton, I realize the schools are up and running again. And maybe there was a *reason* Mother Superior had remained in her tower. I glance at Sherwood's painting that she left on the floor. After all these years, the red eye he painted at the center still remains bright.

"You wanted that tornado to find you here. Didn't you? You were hoping to somehow call it to you with Sherwood's painting—"

I realize this is total crazy talk.

But I also know it seems like no coincidence that the twister came so close to Mother Superior's tower. Without the Stone of Thieves in her hand, and knowing that lately the ghost had been sending people to their deaths, she must've had some nutty idea that the red eye of the twister might help her go back in time. To change the tragedies that she'd unleashed…

But then she saw Creek and I, out in the storm?

And the Stone of Thieves in my hand—

I surprise myself by grabbing the ruby heart from the floor with my shirt sleeve and crouching down beside Mother Superior, next to Creek. Shaking a little, I hold the stone up to her crook nose. The Stone of Thieves pulses so brightly, her whole face glows crimson.

"Not even the magic of the ruby heart can change your past, Mother Superior," I inform her. "It simply reveals what happened, like a psychic fingerprint. Only you can change the future."

Mother Superior proceeds to dig into her pocket. Immediately, I brace myself, watching Creek's arm muscles snap tight. Who knows what weapon she's got or what she'll attempt to do next? This woman is certifiable. But to my relief, she merely holds out her old PP ring and drops it onto the stone. Eyes flickering, she watches the gold begin to bubble and melt, dribbling down the sides of the stone to the floor. It lies in a puddle there, glistening.

The Dove flitters to the sight of the gold, tilting its head with a peculiar gaze. Strangely, it pecks at my hand.

"It wants the note," Mother Superior glances at me with a sigh.

"And so do I," a low voice cuts in.

19

He's a big man with a barrel chest, his large frame filling the entire doorway. Nearly as tall as Creek in a gray, herringbone suit and shiny, black shoes, I watch in terror as a brutal smile lifts on his lips. With the way his side pocket bulges, it doesn't take a detective to figure out he's packing heat.

"Forget your stupid rocks and paintings." He glares at Mother Superior before his eyes dart to a small, pink book on top of one of her file cabinets. "Give me that note. *And* my daughter's diary."

"B-Bradford?" Mother Superior stutters. "H-Helms—"

"Barrett Worth now, bitch," he hisses.

He removes the gun from his suit jacket and aims it straight at my head. Nearby, every muscle in Creek's body is so tight I can almost hear them snapping. But I'm praying he won't step in the line of fire—if someone has to go tonight, I'd rather it be me.

"I want Skyler's journal. You can't fool me—you took it before the police came to investigate last week. And Sherwood's last note," the man says, waving his gun for emphasis. "Or *she* dies."

I know I'm a goner anyway...

This asshole is going to kill us all, even if we give him what he wants. I may come from a privileged household, but I can still tell when a man has a massacre on his mind.

Scared witless, all at once I realize this note in my hand must have Bradford Helm's fingerprints on it. And if Skyler Worth was actually his daughter, then he must've had a secret double life all along that Creek and Caroline didn't know about. Skyler's journal probably talks about his drug exploits— we Pinnacle girls know all about blackmailing our fathers to get what we want, the same way I used to threaten my dad to expose his secrets for money. I shoot a terrified glance at Creek, before my vision becomes a black blur—

Within seconds, I'm flattened beneath Mother Superior's black habit and hefty weight. Her entire being covers me as I hear a shot fire. Blood explodes from her shoulder, splattering onto my body, but instead of squinting in pain, her eyes are all fierce...courage.

She took a bullet for me! Perhaps in some kind of final death wish. Yet every ounce of my being cries out for Creek. As more shots are fired and I struggle to roll out from underneath Mother Superior's body to see what happened to him, I hear a horrific crash.

To my shock, I see Creek has his stepfather pinned to the floor beneath a metal filing cabinet he'd knocked over. It has several bullet holes in the side, and Creek's sitting on top of it with the pistol in his hand pointed at his stepfather's head.

Within inches of Bradford's fingers is Skyler Worth's pink diary, sprawled open. Across the pages are long lists of names in girlish handwriting.

Creek leans down to pick up the notebook, flipping through it and glancing at me.

"Customers," he sighs, giving his stepfather a kick with his heel whenever he tries to wriggle. "From the elite homes in Indian Hill, I bet. What were you dealing this time, Brad? Designer cocaine? A more elegant heroin? Whatever it was, your daughter kept notes on her fat cat daddy to get her way, didn't she? Funny, you never told us about your other family. How very…unsurprising."

He tosses the pink diary aside and slips down to throw off the filing cabinet from his stepfather's back with a crash. The man's arms and legs are splayed in awkward directions, like some of his bones are broken. Then Creek crouches down and points the pistol at Bradford's head, execution style.

So much smoke is rising from the ruby heart on the floor that I dropped when I fell that it fills the room with an eye-stinging haze. Bradford Helms begins to cough.

"Don't shoot!" he cries, hacking. "W-we'll share profits! Just like I always promised you, Creek. I have millions. *Millions*—"

Creek gazes for a second at the angry plume of smoke coming from the Stone of Thieves. Though I can tell by the way his jaw slices back and forth that he'd love nothing more than to put a bullet in this man's head, his eyes meet mine. His hand creases white from strain, every ounce of will he has holding him back from pulling that trigger, and the veins on his temples are about to burst. The moans of Mother Superior clutching the gunshot wound to her shoulder fill the room with a despondent sound like a mournful ghost.

I'd be the last person on earth to blame Creek right now if he blasted that man's head apart. And I'd gladly go to my death lying in court—or anywhere else—just to protect him.

But I also know that this is the greatest test of Creek's life. The moment he decides which one wins: his rage, which ironically makes him just like Bradford, or his future with *me*.

Swallowing hard, I can't tell him who to be. That decision comes from what's in his heart…

And I tremble all over, watching Creek's hand begin to shake. His anger is every bit as intense as always, yet it seems as though the fate of his soul rides on whether he pulls that trigger. For a fleeting moment, Creek's eyes transform into the coldest, glacier-blue I've ever seen as they check mine.

"Death would be too good for you, asshole," Creek whispers in a tone of rough gravel. He steps his boot on his Bradford Helms' neck and leans down to brush the barrel of the gun against his cheek.

"I could have killed you that day," he hisses. "The day you murdered my mother. And believe me, it would be nothing for me to kill you right now." Creek inhales a long, deep breath, managing not to cough from the smoke-filled air. "But with your fingerprints on that note and the information in your daughter's diary, plus Mother Superior's testimony and mine, you'll be locked up for the rest of your miserable life in a six-by-eight-foot cell. Who will you lie to then, huh?" Creek jiggles the gun against his check with relish. "Something tells me you'll have plenty of time to rehearse your bullshit to the walls. Until then, nighty-night *Brad*."

With a swift, pistol whip to the head, Creek renders his stepfather unconscious.

Slowly, Mother Superior gathers her thick legs from beneath her and attempts to get up. I rush to her side and take her by the arm to help her till she's able to stand.

"We have to get you to a hospital!" I gasp.

But her eyes are strangely driven—as electric and focused as they used to appear whenever she was about to issue some edict during our assemblies at Pinnacle. I'm certain her body, if not her brain, must be in shock from the gunshot wound. Yet to my bafflement, she yanks Sherwood's last note for Caroline from my hand and holds it out to the dove, which had been perched nearby on the statue of Saint Francis. Immediately, the bird seizes it and flutters to the windowsill. Mother Superior breaks from my grip and shuffles to the window to open it.

"No!" I cry. "Th-The fingerprints. The evidence—"

"Let her," Creek interrupts sternly. He steps over to wrap his big arm around me and gives me a squeeze. "Caroline deserves to receive her last letter from Sherwood," he whispers. "From her best friend. We have plenty of other evidence."

Tears flow down my cheeks in a stream. Clasping my hands in restraint, I allow Mother Superior to open the window a crack with her one good arm. Her gaze is completely focused, despite the fact that she's bleeding hard enough that droplets fall to the floor.

"Goodbye Bright Eyes," she whispers, nodding at the bird as it disappears with the note into the night.

Mother Superior's knowledge of the old, faithful dove's name makes me realize she'd probably read some of Caroline's journal entries during her years at school.

I step away from Creek's embrace to pick up the ruby heart from the floor with my sleeve. Setting it down, smoldering, into the goblet on the desk again, I watch for a moment as it radiates within the pewter like a hot coal. Then both Creek and I join Mother Superior as she gazes at the moonlight glinting over the spires at Pinnacle.

For a while she simply stands there, clutching the wound on her shoulder, lost in thought. I brace myself, wanting to give her a little space, yet prepared for her to faint from her injuries at any moment. In a strange gesture, however, Mother Superior begins to carefully remove the head pieces of her habit—coif, bandeau, and all—and folds them slowly with her one hand into a neat square, setting them onto her desk. Plucking out bobby pins, she lets her long gray hair spill to her shoulders. When she leans out the window for a moment, my muscles tense, fearing she might try to jump, and Creek swiftly holds out his arm just in case. But instead, she merely waves to the moon.

"Tell my sister Evangeline I'm coming home," she says quietly.

She takes a deep breath, appearing smaller than I remember her, and gives the pale moon one last wave.

"I imagine she'll be expecting me."

There's a huge pile of leaves, branches and old wood burning beside the shore of Bender Lake this morning, with flames high enough to lick the sky.

For once, the fire hasn't been sparked by one of the TNT Twin's explosions or a cannon-shooting game gone awry. It's autumn now, and everyone at Turtle Shores has gathered the stray brush and discarded plywood and crates from around their trailers and wagons to the sands of Bender Lake. This bonfire is our memorial to celebrate our thoughts and memories, backwoods style, of Caroline Gust and her star-crossed lover Sherwood Flynn. All around us, the hardwood trees are starting to become bright with orange and crimson leaves, reflected in the still waters of Bender Lake. But that's not the only thing that's shining brightly.

For some reason, the Stone of Thieves has grown warm in my pocket. It's been dark and cold for months now, and I'm standing beside Creek in a black lace dress and heels, borrowed from my dear friend Brandi. She's here too, along with Dooley on her black leather hip, as well as my parents, Lorraine, the Colonel, Bixby, and the TNT Twins. All of us are wearing dark dresses or suits, and it brings tears to my eyes to see how hard everyone has tried to make themselves look nice for this special event. Granny Tinker is standing in front of the small crowd on this mist-shrouded morning by the lake, wearing her long, black velvet gown and top hat and her crimson, lace-up boots, preparing to say a few words that will hopefully bring us peace. Nevertheless, the ruby heart keeps throbbing in my pocket. I pull it out and see it flash in the glow of the fire.

The moment I do, I spy an older woman walking slowly in the sand toward the bonfire. She has long gray hair and a loose black dress over her wide frame that flows awkwardly with her shuffling steps.

"Well if it ain't the devil," Granny Tinker remarks with a sly smile as the woman approaches. Everyone turns their heads in the direction of the sound that the woman's thick feet make as they churn in the sand. "Glad you could make it, Annabelle Lee Tinker."

Granny's words knock the breath out of me.

It's in that moment that I realize Granny wasn't calling her crystal ball Annabelle Lee last spring and summer for no reason. All along, she was talking to her *sister*—

The former Mother Superior, who resigned from my old boarding school after convalescing from her gunshot wound in the hospital.

Clearly, they both must've grown up as white trash girls together a long time ago in Turtle Shores. But one chose a straight-laced life of religion and status to overcome the ache and uncertainty of poverty. While the other embraced the folks at Turtle Shores and blossomed into their leader, dispensing her uncanny wisdom with Traveller style.

No one around the bonfire seems a bit bothered by Annabelle Lee's return, and I sigh deeply and lean my head on Creek's shoulder. I guess Turtle Shores has a way of offering everyone a new start. After all, this place is famous for being a haven for the lost and confused, including me and my dad when we first came here. Yet it also provides the chance to leave what's no longer working in people's lives, in order to find their true home.

Granny must have known, in her usual mysterious and spooky way, that the winds were about to shift in her older sister's life.

And Annabelle Lee's not the only one who's experienced big changes lately.

I squeeze Creek's hand and glance up into his eyes.

They're different now, those blue eyes of the man I love. More at peace. Yet he's also more *Creek* than I've ever known. There's a piece that was missing from his heart that's been returned to him, after all we've been through together and learned.

It doesn't hurt that justice has finally been served as well.

Because of Creek's and the former Mother Superior's testimony, the local paper reported that Bradford Helms' federal trial will begin next month in Cincinnati, where he'd been living under an assumed name in Indian Hill and dealing a designer methamphetamine called "skyrocket" to the social elite. Before his arrest on the night we were at Pinnacle, he'd become extraordinarily wealthy and could buy off top politicians and law enforcement alike. But based on new evidence, the F.B.I. will not only be prosecuting him for drug trafficking but also for the murders of Caroline Gust and Sherwood Flynn, with Creek and the former Mother Superior expected to be star witnesses. And although the investigation is still ongoing, preliminary DNA results prove within 99% accuracy that Creek is indeed Sherwood Alastair Flynn V's son. As the last remaining male heir to the Flynn banking family, that means Creek is entitled to all that Sherwood Flynn inherited from his trust fund, and more.

Which makes Creek far more wealthy than me.

And probably richer than God.

But none of that seems to interest Creek right now.

His eyes are too intently focused on an old, weathered box that Granny Tinker holds in her hands.

"Ladies and gentlemen," she clears her throat and announces, regarding everyone around the bonfire with a stern gaze, "we are here today to never forget."

She opens the lid of the box and holds up a tarnished bracelet and a small bouquet of dried forget-me-nots.

I immediately become a puddle, tears trickling down my cheeks. I know forget-me-nots had a special meaning between Sherwood and his beloved grandfather, a reminder to choose passion over a mediocre life and to live as vibrantly as possible. But now, they're a memorial to all that Caroline and Sherwood had dreamed of, too—and to their brave spirits and a love that refused to quit. To Sherwood, who risked everything to try and rescue the girl he adored. And to Caroline, who lost her life attempting to spare Creek and

Dooley a destiny of abuse that she no longer wanted them to endure.

Granny Tinker lifts the bracelet and dried flowers higher, snapping me back from my thoughts. "Most of y'all know that I have a way of sensing things and preservin' them inside my wagon," she continues. "Well, years ago, a dove started approachin' me every evenin', just as the sun would go down, with these little items." She studies the wildflowers and jewelry in her fingers. "It all began with this bracelet with a C stamped on it, followed by forget-me-nots and crumpled notes from a young gal named Caroline."

Granny Tinker stares straight at Creek.

"She was a gal of hope, that Caroline," Granny says, as if to remind him. "Even though times were hard fer her, she wanted the best part of herself—her soul—to be preserved in these tokens that she released to the wind. These notes," Granny pulls out an old piece of paper from the box, "were her love letters to the world. Because Caroline truly believed in love, despite the circumstances that caused her downfall. An' she wanted a record of that left somewhere that the bad folks in her life couldn't destroy. So her pet dove brought 'em to me, fer safekeepin'."

Granny takes a few of the dried flowers from the box and tosses them into the fire, where they quickly rise as sparks that fly up in the flames.

"Ol' folks reckon that dust returns to dust," Granny observes. "But that was the unusual thing about Caroline, which y'all can tell from her letters. Her heart was so big and pure—an' alive—that I believe it'll go on forever. Because of her love, she often took the beatings an' abuse that her no-good boyfriend and murderer intended for her children. An' after all she endured, there's one thing I know fer sure— Caroline loved Creek and Dooley more than anythin' in this world. So Dooley, I think it's time fer you to have this."

Granny Tinker steps over to Dooley and hands him Caroline's silver bracelet. She ruffles his ivory hair and cups his chin tenderly for a moment. Dooley nods and slips the bracelet around the neck of his favorite blue, stuffed bunny, the one Creek rescued from their old trailer and returned to him. Then Dooley strokes the bunny's ears and squeezes him tight against his chest, whispering a secret to him like he's an old friend.

And for the first time ever, I see a tear slip down Creek's cheek. He steps over and tells Dooley how much he loves him, and hugs him right then and there.

That's when I see the cracks in the Stone of Thieves in my hand completely fuse together.

It's whole now…

Like Creek.

Creek returns to my side and grasps my hand, clenching it tight. Together, we watch a large plume of smoke rise from the flames in a swirling gust of air. I blink several times, wondering if I'm seeing things. I can't be sure—but to me, it looks like there are the shapes of two lovers entwined who rise up in the morning sky. As the figures go higher and higher, a dove appears that spirals along with them into the golden light of the early morning sun. A small white feather falls at our feet, and when I glance at Creek, I notice he's staring in the bird's direction. From in the distance, I hear the dove call softly as the figures drift away on thin wafts of smoke.

"And as for Sherwood Flynn, the love of Caroline's life—well, his love fer her knew no bounds," Granny Tinker continues. "Even after all this time, his final letter to Caroline found its way to my wagon on a dove's wings." Granny rifles through the old box and holds up Sherwood's last note to the small crowd. "That's the thing about true love—it's never wasted. It'll always makes its way back home. So if'n ya'll take anything away from our memorial today, I hope you'll set yer heart to love...and to forgiveness." Granny stares solemnly across the orange flames of the fire at her sister. "Cause heaven knows, you kin never tell when the tides of a person's heart are about to turn."

Everyone around the bonfire is silent for a long time, absorbed in the sacred hush of the moment—a minor miracle for the boisterous folks of Turtles Shores. But then Bixby sneaks a sip of moonshine from a flask inside his coat pocket. Before long, all the men are copying him and swiping drinks, till we hear the loud clanging of a bell.

It's Lorraine, back at the trailer park, ringing to signal breakfast. Simultaneously, the men on the beach erupt into a wild holler.

This is still Bender Lake, after all.

"Well that, my friends, marks the end of our memorial," Granny Tinker says in a steady tone. Her lips rise a little at the predictability of their exuberance. "I expect it's time to head to Lorraine's trailer now fer breakfast. Life goes on, and so must we. But the next chance you get to dance around a bonfire at Turtle Shores, I want y'all to remember the lives of these two souls who fought fer love, the same way we often fight to protect what we have here. May the fire of their memory set yer hearts free."

Granny closes the box and walks slowly around the bonfire to wrap her arm around her big sister. She gives her a gentle squeeze. "Mighty nice to have you back home, Annabelle Lee," she smiles, flashing her gold tooth. "Who knows what trouble we'll get into with the two of us here. First time we been together in Turtle Shores for thirty years. You know what they always say, darlin'. This big ol' world is run by little ol' ladies in black dresses."

Granny laughs loudly, above even the stomping of feet through the sand by people storming toward breakfast. The scent of Lorraine's biscuits and gravy is enough to bring even wild animals running. Yet I have to smile as the echo of Granny's cackle travels its way across the mists of Bender Lake.

Because to me, it sounds like home.

Later that evening, Creek and I cuddle beneath the warmth of the old quilts in our wagon. We're stretched out lazily on the soft bed, our bodies entangled, gazing at the bright colors of Sherwood Flynn's last painting, which shimmers in the candlelight. It hangs on our wall now, the one he created with Caroline of the red eye of the storm. We found the canvas earlier today, leaning against our wagon. A peace offering, I guess, from Annabelle Lee.

Or perhaps her way of apologizing for everything that happened.

Rumor has it she's living quietly in a rusty trailer across the woods from Granny Tinker's wagon. I can only picture what their conversations must be like as they spend time catching up with each other over one of Granny's handpicked herbal teas. And who knows, maybe Granny might even slip Annabelle Lee a spell or two—especially for learning how to open her heart. But I bet Annabelle Lee's medieval art collection had to stay with Pinnacle, along with the proceeds of Sherwood's other paintings. Because something tells me she probably no longer has a dime to her name.

That's okay. Creek and I will look after her.

Why?

That's what folks do for each other at Turtle Shores. And heaven knows, we've made mistakes in life, too, and required our fair share of understanding. I, of all people, needed to dig deep to drum up the strength to forgive Annabelle Lee for her misdeeds as Mother Superior, knowing how difficult it was for Creek when I insisted that he forgive his mom. But for Christ's sake, the woman took a bullet risking her life for me. And at this point, it seems like extending a little mercy is the least I can do for Annabelle Lee. I guess what Creek and I have learned through all of this is that everyone has complex reasons for their actions. And sometimes, if you look hard enough, you just might find that they have a heart, buried deep within their chests, after all.

I twirl Creek's wayward blonde hair between my fingers, relishing the warm glow of the candlelight on his striking features, along with this new-found peace in our lives. A curl of smoke spirals up from a candle, one with a musky, herbal scent created by Granny. Smiling a little, I have to wonder if it includes a spell for enduring love. Yet in spite of the ease I feel right now, the way the candle smoke twirls reminds me of what I saw this morning on the beach. I clear my throat, mustering the courage to approach the subject with Creek.

"Did you, um, *see* them, Creek?" I whisper. "This morning, in the bonfire?"

Creek lies still with his eyes closed. His eyes flutter open a little and he glances at the candle smoke without saying a word. Finally, he nods in silence.

"Do you think that means Sherwood and Caroline are together now, in the hereafter?"

"I figure they always were, Robin," Creek says quietly. "The moment my mom died, I think she joined him straightaway." His lip rises in a soft smile. "And she made it her business to look after me and Dooley, leaving us white feathers as hints. In fact," he steals a glance at me, his eyes twinkling, "I bet my mom helped me to find *you*."

He snuggles tighter against me, his bare skin warm against mine. Even so, something still troubles me. I know I should let these issues rest. And I promise myself I will, just as soon as I glean a few more answers.

"Creek," I say hesitantly, "if you think both of them were together all along, and your mom has been guiding you in her own way, then which one of them was terrorizing Pinnacle? I mean, as a ghost?"

"Neither," Creek replies mysteriously. He sighs.

To my surprise, he tumbles me over in the bed so that he's on top and gazes into my eyes. Tenderly, he brushes a long, curly lock away from my forehead. His eyebrows are creased together and his liquid-blue eyes appear cautious as well as concerned. For a long while he's quiet, as though he doesn't want to hurt me with what he knows.

"You can tell me, Creek," I prompt. "We've been through so much together. You know me—I can take it."

Creek picks up the Stone of Thieves from a small dresser beside our bed. He gazes at the star-like radiance at the center of the ruby, which is entirely smooth now without any cracks.

Running his fingers over the stone's surface for a moment, he clears his throat.

"It was me, baby," he says. "All along. With some awfully dark help from Annabelle Lee."

I have no idea what he's talking about. I'm totally confused now, and his peculiar words make my heart race.

Creek sets the stone back down and takes a deep breath. He cups my cheeks and stares intently into my eyes.

"I'm not going to wake up swinging in the middle of the night anymore," he promises. "You were right, Robin. All that rage inside, it was killing me—and it came between us. And that's what I saw that night in the red eye of the tornado. When I tore away from you and stood before the storm, I-I had a vision. And it was like looking into a mirror."

"Mirror of what?"

"Of *me*. All I saw in the radiance of the twister was my own reflection, staring back at me. I was the rage. I was the fury. I know that sounds crazy, Robin. But when the magical Stone of Thieves came into our lives, it's power was stoked by my own anger and it took on some kind of otherworldly form that got twisted through Annabelle Lee. And it wasn't going to rest," he points at the smoke drifting up from the candle in our wagon, "until I did. Till I finally let the anger go."

"So *you* were the energy that was going after those people?"

I have to admit I'm scared witless—chilled by this strange and destructive power that was somehow manifested through Creek.

Creek shakes his head slowly.

"Not entirely. I never touched…anyone," he admits. "And

something about the darkness in their own hearts brought these fates upon themselves. But I'm not going to lie to you, Robin. Granny Tinker's the most magical woman I've ever known, and Annabelle Lee is her *sister*—with a heavy number of enchantments in her own right, whether she owns up to them or not. I think Annabelle Lee was so overcome by guilt and her desire to make the past right again that her desperation magically used my spirit's anger as a conduit to make that justice happen. She might've looked like Mother Superior on the outside, but on the inside, she was pure sorceress, even though it was probably unconscious. Annabelle Lee simply couldn't stop herself from unleashing that dark magic until she knew the past was brought to rest."

"C-could something like this ever happen again?"

A cool, autumn breeze drifts in through our open window, as though clearing the air.

Creek gazes at me. There are no obvious answers in his eyes. Only the love I see that he has for me.

"Robin—I love you," he whispers. "And I'd never do anything to hurt you, *ever*. When the red eye of the twister showed me Sherwood's and Caroline's last meeting, how much they really loved each other, and we saw in the ruby heart that Sherwood tried to save her, well, all that anger finally left me. No dark magic can capitalize on my rage again, because it's gone. And I don't think it's ever coming back."

He leans over and rolls his body against mine, nuzzling my cheek. "The storm's over, baby," he promises. "We're safe now."

"It wasn't your fault," I say gently to Creek, caressing his soft hair as my heart breaks for him. "Anyone would've carried that burden of anger after what you saw happen to your mom," I insist. "You're not responsible for how it got twisted by a weird magic that demanded justice. You're only responsible for how you go forward now. Will you tell Dooley? I mean, the truth about Caroline not being—"

"Dooley will *always* be my brother, Robin," Creek corrects.

I nod in agreement. That's the truth, biology be damned.

"Creek, there's one other thing—"

"You talk too much!" he smiles, running his hand down my cheek and kissing my neck.

"But you're rich now," I remind him. "What are you going to do with all that money? With the rest of your life?" I turn and run my fingers over the scar I carved into his bicep that says *Partners*. "Go into banking? Meet the Flynn family for Thanksgiving this year? You could invite the TNT Twins. They'd literally be a blast—"

Creek laughs a little and shakes his head, keeping an eye on the drifting candle smoke. "It's okay not to know everything, Robin," he scolds gently. "To let life unfold the way maybe it's supposed to for a while. Somehow, I think those decisions will make themselves when when it's the right time to make them. And until then, all that matters to me now is that we're home."

He gazes at me, looking more content than I've ever witnessed, his blue eyes warm and…happy. Happy to be with *me*. Then he picks up the ruby stone from the dresser again and stares at it for a moment, studying its perfectly smooth surface and heart shape, the way its facets reflect myriad angles of light like a crimson flame. The ragged scar on his cheek crinkles into that familiar, dagger smile.

"But one thing I do know for certain," Creek says, lifting up a pillow from on our bed. Beneath it, to my astonishment, I spot two airline tickets…

To *Italy*, of all places.

"It's high time we return this stone to the gypsies. Don't you agree, Mrs. Flynn?"

His eyes sparkle, and he kisses me, long and slow, like we belong to one another. Not just for now, but for eternity. The same way the Stone of Thieves will always be the core of the beating heart of the gypsies.

And of course, my answer to him is yes.

ABOUT THE AUTHOR

USA TODAY bestselling author Diane J. Reed writes happily ever afters with a touch of magic that make you believe in the power of love. Her stories feed the soul with outlaws, mavericks, and dreamers who have big hearts under big skies and dare to risk all for those they cherish. Because love is more than a feeling—it's the magic that changes everything.

To get the latest on new releases, sign up for Diane J. Reed's newsletter at dianejreed.com.

www.ingramcontent.com/pod-product-compliance
Lightning Source LLC
Chambersburg PA
CBHW031454260626
47154CB00017B/2689